Holiday Folding Stories

Storytelling and Origami Together For Holiday Fun

by Christine Petrell Kallevig

photographs by Terey Page

International

P. O. Box 470505, Broadview Heights, Ohio 44147

Storytime Ink International
P. O. Box 470505, Broadview Heights, Ohio 44147

ISBN 0-9628769-1-7

Illustrations by Christine Petrell Kallevig.

First Edition
10 9 8 7 6 5 4 3 2 1
Printed in the United States of America

Library of Congress Catalog Card Number: 91-068161

ACKNOWLEDGMENTS
Procedures for folding the heart and the Christmas tree were learned from Toshie
Takahama in *The Joy of Origami*, (Shufunotomo/Japan Publications, 1985), p. 51, 53

Procedure for folding the lotus blossom was learned from Isao Honda in *The World
Of Origami*, (Japan Publication Trading Co., 1965).

Procedure for folding the bunny was learned from Kazuo Kobayashi and Makoto
Yamaguchi in *Origami for Parties*, (Kodansha International, 1987), p. 20.

Procedure for folding the basket was learned from Toshie Takahama in *Quick &
Easy Origami*, (Kodansha International, 1988), p. 46.

The author expresses appreciation to...

Carol Clancy, for her astute editing and careful proof-reading.

Emily, Jackie, David, and Paul, for their limitless enthusiasm and photogenic joy.

Terey Page, for her creative and sensitive photography skills.

Jim, David, and Paul Kallevig for their help, patience, and support.

o the ancient revelers who found cause to celebrate, creating festivals and holidays we still enjoy. May we always honor their traditions, while discovering new ones of our own.

TABLE OF CONTENTS

Holidays, stories, and origami...
A great way to celebrate!

When can three old things be blended together to form something new? The answer: when storytelling is combined with origami (Japanese paperfolding) in honor of ancient holiday traditions. The result: Holiday Storigami!

It's a simple method. Storytelling + Origami = Storigami. In other words, create a holiday story, then illustrate the events of the story with actual origami folds. When the story is over, a simple, three dimensional holiday symbol is complete. Recalling the sequence of events in the story is the same as recalling the sequence of folds necessary to make the origami holiday figure. Listeners enjoy the experience of delightful new stories and also gain the ability to construct their own holiday creations.

Holidays are ideal occasions to unite origami and storytelling. An example of the compatibility of this combination is seen in the story "A Miracle Happened There", p. 33. It tells about the origin of Hanukkah and the traditional children's symbol, the dreidel. Scholars believe that dreidels were derived from ancient Japanese tops or spinning whorls. In "A Miracle Happened There", the Oriental influence ironically reappears as the paper dreidel is constructed using Japanese paperfolding techniques. The result is a new, harmonious blending of ancient folk arts.

Holiday Storigami also provides a non-materialistic alternative to holiday celebrations. Emphasis is placed on wholesome fun and creative achievement, rather than on short term bursts of electronic pleasure. The enjoyment of Storigami comes from within the listeners as they visualize the scenes presented by the storyteller, painting their mental landscapes with an endless array of individualized colors. Learning how to fold a new origami model is not a momentary thrill, but a pleasure that can be shared with others again and again. Storigami is entertainment that is inexpensive, educational, and results in increased pride and self esteem.

What are the educational benefits of Storigami?

1. **Improved listening skills:** listeners are motivated to pay close attention to the stories.

2. **Opportunities to practice right cerebral hemisphere visualization skills:** listeners imagine the scenes described in the stories and the illustrations represented by the progressive origami folds.

3. **Opportunities to practice left cerebral hemisphere language comprehension skills:** listeners understand the words used to describe story elements such as plot, characters, dialog, and setting.

4. **Emphasis is placed on multi-sensory, integrated whole brain learning techniques:** visual, kinesthetic, and auditory senses all provide the right and left cerebral hemispheres with input, resulting in an atmosphere of whole-brain learning.

5. **Memory enhancement:** achieved through paired associations and multi-sensory presentations.

6. **Improved fine motor skills:** folding and manipulating paper provides practice for eye-hand coordination.

7. **Opportunities to examine and practice spatial relationships:** spatial concepts include right & left, front & back, top & bottom, inside & outside, beside, under, parallel, symmetrical, etc.

8. **Opportunities to practice higher order thinking skills:** optional applications included with each story list ways to improve skills relating to evaluation, synthesis, analysis, and application.

9. **Supplemental material:** the stories complement units in basic subjects such as math, geography, history, art, music, or science.

10. **Opportunities to enhance social skills:** increased self-esteem is a by-product of successfully learning new skills. Ideas for social interactions are provided in the optional applications.

Is previous storytelling or origami experience required?

No! The strength of this system is its simplicity. There are no complicated symbols or specialized terms in the directions. The illustrations were drawn so that beginners with no previous origami experience can fold with success and confidence. Optional introductory statements are offered for storytellers who stumble over the "getting started" phase.

But please read the next section called, "Before you begin." It is loaded with tips based on experiences gained from the field-testing phase of this book.

Who should practice Storigami?

Art teachers who would like to introduce origami in an entertaining and non-threatening way to inexperienced paper folders.

Children's librarians who would like to combine an inexpensive paper craft with literature that American children will both enjoy and identify.

Storytellers who enjoy new and unusual props to peak their listeners' interest.

Activity therapists who are challenged by groups composed of individuals with diverse interests and levels of sophistication.

Recreation, troop and club leaders who organize and present wholesome activities on limited budgets.

Origami specialists who present workshops to novice folders and would like to introduce basic folding techniques in an interesting and effective format.

Parents, grandparents, uncles & aunts who would like to spice up family activities with a fun and inexpensive new hobby.

Teachers seeking to supplement basic subject matter with whole-language, whole-brain methodology within their intellectually and culturally diverse classrooms.

**For best results,
follow these guidelines:**

1. Match the story activities to your group.

2. Pre-fold the origami figure.

3. Have required materials prepared.

4. Be familiar with the story.

5. Enhance the story with holiday history.

6. Plan a response to reluctant folders.

7. Expect and accept imperfect first folds.

8. Understand folding directions.

Match the story activities to your group.

Every story in this book features a different origami model. The stories incorporate actual holiday traditions, some modern, some historical, that can be enjoyed by virtually all age groups. The origami figures were selected because they are symbolic of the featured holidays and are among the easiest and least complex to learn. Success with these simple models help non-folders feel confident and comfortable with elementary paper-folding techniques. However, even with these basic models, varying levels of difficulty exist. It is important to select follow-up activities that match your group's abilities, ages, interests, and developmental levels.

It is perfectly acceptable to tell the holiday stories without teaching the origami folds, particularly if you have time constraints or your group size is too large or too young to effectively learn the folding techniques.

Pre-fold the origami figure for most effective storytelling.

The most pleasing origami models are constructed with clean, sharp folds where the paper edges are precisely aligned. Expert folders can accomplish this feat without the support of a hard, flat surface. But the rest of us need a flat surface to make accurate creases. Unfortunately, hard flat surfaces are not always available or practical in storytelling locations.

To overcome this presentation problem and to be able to tell the story smoothly without taking excessive folding time, it is *essential* to pre-fold the model featured in your selected story. Then, as you approach each step, the folds will simply snap into place. You will not fumble with the paper nor suddenly forget what to do. Your story delivery will be confident and dynamic as you concentrate on the story text and your group's responses.

Have all required materials ready before you begin.

The title page for each story includes a photograph of the featured origami model, a brief description of the story, and a list of materials required for the presentation of the story. If you plan to teach the model or use the story to support other activities, you will need several squares of paper for each group member. Plan to have plenty of paper for practice or mistakes.

Be familiar with the text.

Experienced storytellers will want to memorize the stories for their presentations. But others will want to refer to the book as they present the stories. For this reason, the photos of the featured origami figures are placed on the title pages *only*, so that when the story is open in front of a group, the listeners will not be able to see what figure will finally emerge.

This element of surprise makes the stories more intriguing and ironic. Listeners of all ages are delighted when the final figure emerges. As always, story presentations are most effective when the storyteller is very familiar with the material.

Enhance the stories with holiday history.

All of the stories include historical information about the featured holiday or holiday symbol. Listeners are often curious about the origin of our holiday traditions, how long we have been celebrating in a particular manner, and who was responsible for making the holiday popular.

The stories work perfectly as holiday party diversions, but they also fit neatly into a wide variety of subject areas or units of study. Many of the optional activities have been labeled according to particular memory or thinking skills for the convenience of those required to write goal directed lesson plans or for those who are simply interested in promoting these abilities. The skills and subjects addressed by the optional activities are listed in the index.

Not all of the activities are appropriate for all groups and are not designed to be presented together. They are merely suggestions for the storyteller or are intended to spark a new idea for a creative application.

Areas have been designated in these sections for logging your own applications or making notes about the response of your group to the activities you tried. It is often helpful to note presentation details so that future planning can be facilitated.

Plan a response for reluctant folders.

Some children and adults are so afraid of ruining the paper, making mistakes or attempting new activities that they won't even try. They exclaim loudly, "I *can't* do it!"

One way to overcome this reluctance is to avoid distributing practice paper until the story is finished and the folding sequence has been reviewed. This helps the group feel confident about remembering what comes next and eliminates worry related to forgetfulness.

Discourage participants from folding along as you first tell the story. This distracts other group members and reduces the folder's ability to associate the story events with the progressive folding steps. Learning would therefore be less effective.

Another successful technique is to fold each step together as a group, saying often, "Yes! That's right. This is easy." Affirming that the task is not hard and publicly praising successful efforts sets a positive tone for beginners.

Always relate the folding steps to the story events, reinforcing the associations for memory enhancement. When a folder can not remember what step comes next, instead of simply telling him, say, "What did Martin see flying in the woods?" or "Who did Queen Hen take the eggs to?" When these associations between the story and the folds are emphasized, long term memory is improved.

Reluctant folders are reassured when a casual or humorous presentation style is emphasized. Too much perfection or seriousness promotes folding reluctance. The stories are whimsical and should be presented with a light-hearted tone.

Expect and accept imperfect folds from beginners.

New paper folders sometimes feel overwhelmed by the experience. During the first folding trial, concentrate on following the sequence of steps necessary to create the model. Most beginners are pleased with their results and surprised that paperfolding really is easy. They immediately want to make another one.

During second and third attempts, begin to emphasize the quality and sharpness of the folds, suggesting that the model will be more attractive when all of the edges and corners are lined up exactly during every step. Encourage them to slow down. As beginning folders become more confident, give them smaller and smaller squares of paper to fold. This increases precision and sustains an element of surprise or challenge throughout the practicing phase.

Avoid criticizing lop-sided or ragged first results. Instead, say, "Yes! I *knew* you could do it! Let's make another one to share. This time, try lining up the edges before you crease the paper. That might help it stand up better."

How to make the origami figures:

1. Every story includes a summary of folding directions. Use these directions when pre-folding the origami figure. Then go back to see where the folds occur in the story. Always use a pre-folded model to tell the stories. (Simply unfold the completed model so that all the necessary creases will already be there.)

2. All figures in this book, except the Halloween BOO! Machine, start as squares. It is important that the squares be exactly the same length on all sides. Squares can easily be made from rectangular paper by folding a corner down (as shown) and trimming away the excess:

3. Origami paper can be purchased pre-cut in a variety of beautiful colors and textures. However, all of the figures in this book can be made very successfully with paper you already have in your home, office or classroom. Experiment with different weights and textures for the most satisfying results.

4. Use a hard, flat surface when making initial folds. Line up edges and corners precisely and hold in place before you crease.

5. Follow each step in the directions in the order they are given. Only after you are very proficient in making a figure, should you attempt to alter the established technique.

6. Explanation of symbols:

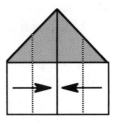

Shaded areas indicate that the back side of the paper is now facing up.

Arrows point to the direction of the fold.

Dotted or dashed lines mark where the next crease will be.

Solid lines indicate existing creases, folds, or edges.

Let your imagination sail away in this simple little boat. Folding directions begin on page 14.

MORE TO DISCOVER

About the story:

Michael asks, "What if the world really is flat?" He compares himself to Christopher Columbus and sets sail on an imaginary trip to the edge of the Earth, finally realizing that he, too, can become a famous discoverer one day.

Recommended ages: Listening only - age 3 through adult.
Listening and folding - age 7 through adult.

Required materials:

One square of paper at least six inches on each side, folded into a boat and then completely unfolded for storytelling.

Optional introductory statement:

I'm going to tell you a story about a boy who admires Christopher Columbus so much that he pretends what it might be like to lead a great exploration to the edge of the world. Watch carefully as I fold this square (hold up the unfolded origami boat) into various shapes. This is called origami, or Japanese paperfolding. The name of the story is "More to Discover".

More To Discover

Michael leaped off the school bus and sliced his narrow shoulders through groups of giggling students, their backpacks and book bags bulging with crumpled math papers and Bologna sandwiches. He dashed into school, slowing to a fast walk only when he passed the "NO RUNNING" sign posted outside the principal's office. No, he wasn't rushing to do last night's forgotten homework. And he didn't have to use the bathroom or deliver any special messages. It was nearly Columbus Day, Michael's favorite holiday, and of all the kids in his class, he had been chosen to act the part of Christopher Columbus in their Columbus Day play.

For as long as Michael could remember, his teachers talked about Christopher Columbus in the fall. They made ships and drew navigation maps, but mostly he loved to hear the story of Columbus' first voyage, especially the part about how the superstitious sailors feared that the world was flat and that if they sailed far enough out into the unchartered seas, they would be attacked by terrible monsters before falling off the edge of the world. Even though Christopher Columbus ruined this great monster myth by proving once and for all that the world was as round as the most educated scholars thought it was, Michael still admired him. After all, who else had become so famous by making one of history's biggest mistakes? Imagine believing that America was the Orient!

When Michael goofed, nobody ever awarded him with piles of gold or gave him a special title like Admiral of the Ocean Sea. Oh no...his mistakes, like not paying attention or not doing homework, usually earned Michael an award of doing extra math problems or missing recess. But Columbus messed up big time, told everyone in the world about it, insisted he was right to the day he died, and never had to miss even one minute of recess. No wonder the guy had a national holiday...pulling off a stunt like that!

Although Michael was smart enough to know better, he thought that a flat world shaped like this *(hold an unfolded square of paper in your palm)* might make sense if there were tall mountains like this *(demonstrate with fold #1)* surrounding all the sides, blocking the oceans from pouring out and flooding the rest of the solar system.

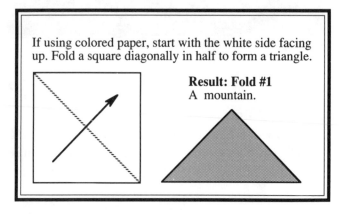

If using colored paper, start with the white side facing up. Fold a square diagonally in half to form a triangle.

Result: Fold #1
A mountain.

And if there were tall mountains, there would naturally be mysterious creatures living in them, like eagles that had mountain lion heads or serpents with volcanic lava boiling in their bellies. And sooner or later, a determined explorer like Christopher Columbus would sail to the edge of the earth to climb the mountains in search of gold for his king and riches deep enough to last his lifetime. He would surely carry special darts like this *(demonstrate with fold #2)* to fend off the mountain creatures and protect his crew.

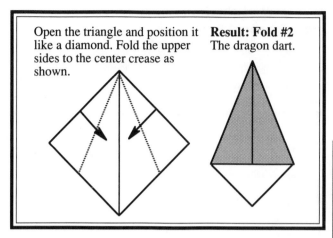

Open the triangle and position it like a diamond. Fold the upper sides to the center crease as shown.

Result: Fold #2
The dragon dart.

At night, the crew would probably sleep in tents like this *(demonstrate with fold #3)*.

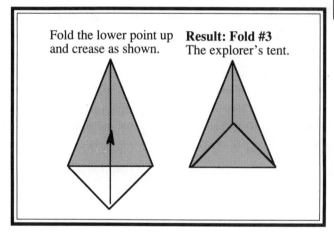

Fold the lower point up and crease as shown.

Result: Fold #3
The explorer's tent.

And wear uniforms with special hats like this *(demonstrate with fold #4)*.

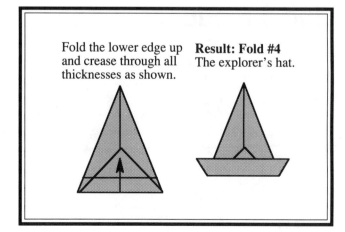

Fold the lower edge up and crease through all thicknesses as shown.

Result: Fold #4
The explorer's hat.

The whole crew would wear this hat except for the captain...no, the admiral. Because he was in charge of the exploration, the Admiral of the Ocean Sea would wear a special hat with the corners tucked in like this *(demonstrate with fold #5)*.

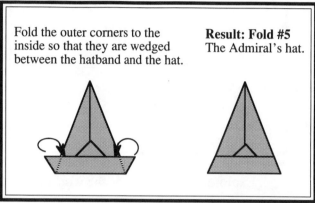

Fold the outer corners to the inside so that they are wedged between the hatband and the hat.

Result: Fold #5
The Admiral's hat.

It wouldn't be smart to endanger their big ocean ships in the shallow waters around the mountains, so they would sail from mountain to mountain in little boats like this *(demonstrate with fold #6)*.

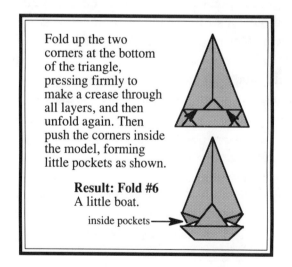

Fold up the two corners at the bottom of the triangle, pressing firmly to make a crease through all layers, and then unfold again. Then push the corners inside the model, forming little pockets as shown.

Result: Fold #6
A little boat.

inside pockets —→

Of course, a flat earth would probably be very unsteady with lots of hurricanes that would easily capsize their little boats like this: *(The little boat is not self-supporting. Let it fall over as a demonstration of its unsteadiness.)* It wouldn't take any time for a powerful gust to break the sail like this *(demonstrate with fold #7).*

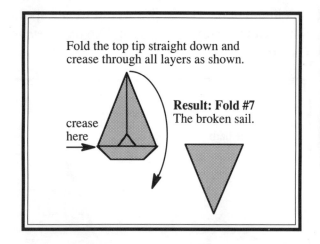

Fold the top tip straight down and crease through all layers as shown.

crease here

Result: Fold #7
The broken sail.

Explorers at the edge of the world can't just run to a telephone to call a shipbuilder whenever they have trouble. Even Columbus and his crew, while exploring our round world, had to know how to survive without any help. They especially had to know how to fix their own ships. In fact, of Columbus' first three ships, the largest ship, the Santa Maria, ran into a shallow reef outside of the island of Haiti and was wrecked even worse than this little boat *(hold up the crippled model).* The smaller ships, the Nina and Pinta, were the only two to sail back to Spain on Columbus' first voyage of discovery.

If Michael was the Admiral of the Ocean Sea, he would fix his boat by making it sturdier. He would fold the broken sail up like this and tuck it inside so that it stayed there without flopping around. *(Demonstrate with fold #8).*

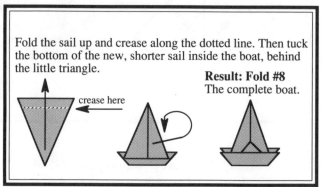

Fold the sail up and crease along the dotted line. Then tuck the bottom of the new, shorter sail inside the boat, behind the little triangle.

crease here

Result: Fold #8
The complete boat.

And then he would travel from place to place, just like Columbus sailed from island to island. He'd face the unknown, make new discoveries, and tell everyone in the world about his new ideas. If they liked what he had to share, perhaps there would even be a holiday for him one day. Yes, he could see it all now...move over, Christopher Columbus. Make room for Michael Day! Or _____ Day, or _____ Day, or _____ Day. *(Fill in the blanks with the names of your listeners).* There's more to discover! There's always more to discover.

Summary of folding directions:

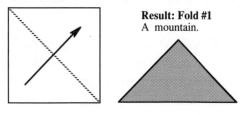

If using colored paper, start with the white side facing up. Fold a square diagonally in half to form a triangle.

Result: Fold #1
A mountain.

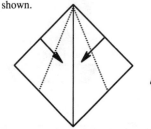

Open the triangle and position it like a diamond. Fold the upper sides to the center crease as shown.

Result: Fold #2
The dragon dart.

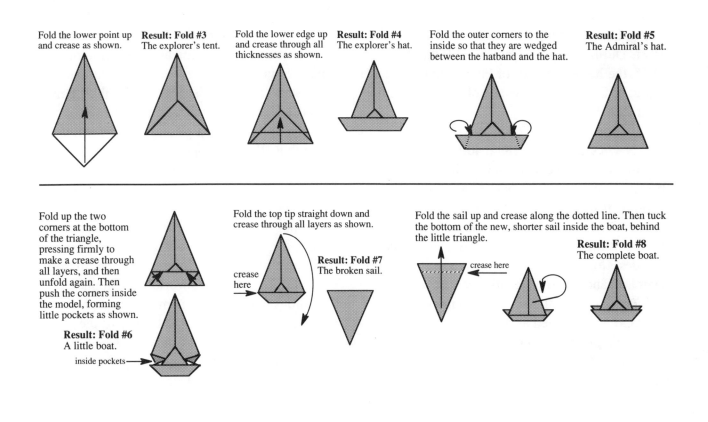

Fold the lower point up and crease as shown.

Result: Fold #3
The explorer's tent.

Fold the lower edge up and crease through all thicknesses as shown.

Result: Fold #4
The explorer's hat.

Fold the outer corners to the inside so that they are wedged between the hatband and the hat.

Result: Fold #5
The Admiral's hat.

Fold up the two corners at the bottom of the triangle, pressing firmly to make a crease through all layers, and then unfold again. Then push the corners inside the model, forming little pockets as shown.

Result: Fold #6
A little boat.

inside pockets

Fold the top tip straight down and crease through all layers as shown.

crease here

Result: Fold #7
The broken sail.

Fold the sail up and crease along the dotted line. Then tuck the bottom of the new, shorter sail inside the boat, behind the little triangle.

crease here

Result: Fold #8
The complete boat.

HOLIDAY HISTORY

Columbus Day Celebrations

The first Columbus Day observance occurred on October 12, 1792, 300 years after Columbus first laid eyes on the New World. A social and political club of New York, The Order of Columbia, also referred to as the Society of Saint Tammany, held a dinner in New York City, and unveiled a fourteen foot high statue of Columbus. The world's first public monument to Columbus was also dedicated on that 300th anniversary in Baltimore, Maryland. It was a 44 foot column of brick, covered with cement and decorated with a marble slab.

Although these were the first Columbus Day celebrations, Christopher Columbus had already been honored in other ways. A college in New York, formerly known as King's, decided to call itself Columbia College as early as 1784. In 1786, the new capital of South Carolina was called Columbia. Also in 1786, the Columbian Magazine was founded. In 1787, the song "Columbia", by Timothy Dwight, was published. The federal government was established in 1791 on land called "the Territory of Columbia".

In 1846, Columbus was memorialized in Washington D. C. with a marble sculpture showing Columbus holding aloft a globe. Later, a bronze statue was erected in that city in 1864. Boston erected a small statue of Columbus as a boy in Louisberg Square in 1849 and again in 1871. During the great Centennial Exhibition in 1876, the Italian citizens of Philadelphia built a statue of Columbus at the site of the exhibition in Fairmont Park.

On October 12, 1892, 400 years after Columbus' discovery, President Benjamin Harrison designated October 12 as a general holiday. It was known as Columbus Day, Discovery Day, or Landing Day. New York City led off the events of October 1892 with five days of parades, floats, fireworks, speeches, military marches, and navel pageants that attracted a million visitors to the city. That same year, Chicago was selected as the site of the World's Columbian Exposition of 1892. The exhibition opened in May 1983 and 24 million people attended, the largest crowd for any single event in the history of the world to that point. Columbus was recognized throughout the world. By this time there were 28 major public monuments to Columbus in the US, ten in the Caribbean, two in Mexico, five in South America, and 19 in Europe.

Towns and cities in every South American country bear a version of the name of Columbus as does the country of Columbia. Over 80 portraits hang in museums throughout the world. More than a dozen museums contain various sized models of the Nina, the Pinta, and the Santa Maria. The Columbus Memorial Library in the Pan American Building in Washington contains the largest collection of source material and official documents on the American republics.

A 1988 survey determined that there were as many as 65 political locations in the United States using variations of "Columbus" in 37 states and the District of Columbia. This includes 50 cities (the largest is Columbus, Ohio, population 632,910 and the smallest is Columbus, Illinois, population 92), nine counties, five townships, and one Air Force base. This does not include natural geographical places such as rivers, capes, mountains, or lakes; nor the seemingly endless numbers of streets, avenues, circles, bridges, companies, or parks also bearing the Columbus name. In the entire English speaking world, Christopher Columbus has given his name to more places than any other person in the history of the world, with the exception only of Queen Victoria. In the United States, only George Washington has more places named for him.

Colorado was the first state to officially celebrate Columbus Day in 1905, thanks largely to the determined efforts of Angelo Noce, a first generation Italian printer from Denver. He traveled throughout the country to lobby for Columbus Day holidays. Columbus Day was an official holiday in fifteen states by 1910. It wasn't until 1934 that President Franklin D. Roosevelt issued a proclamation asking all 48 states to observe October 12 as a national holiday.

The US Congress officially made Columbus Day a legal national holiday in 1971. It is now observed on the second Monday in October.

Optional applications for "More To Discover"

1. After telling the story, review Michael's flat earth fantasy, from the flat piece of paper through the complete construction of the little boat. Emphasize the correct sequence of folds, giving each step its name from the story: high mountain, protective dart, explorer's tent, etc. *(auditory sequential memory)*. Reconstruct the boat for the group, asking the group to identify each step *(visual sequential memory)*. With younger or less attentive groups, construct the boat again with a fresh, unfolded piece of paper. Ask the group to actually teach you what to build, step by step. Emphasize the need to line up the edges as you fold, pressing the creases firmly and completely. Only after the group is confident about the folding procedure, should you distribute squares of paper. Fold together step by step *(kinesthetic memory)* or allow independent folding, assisting only when needed *(synthesis)*.

2. Decorate the sail with a red cross, draw boards to represent planks in the body of the boat, and shape the little triangle to represent Columbus, adding appropriate facial and clothing details *(application)*. Ask the group to predict where the markings would fall on an unfolded square of paper. Gather reasons for their decisions. Unfold the decorated boats to discover the real answers. Refold to observe the decorations fall back into place *(analysis, synthesis, evaluation)*.

3. Fold the boats from various sized squares to represent Columbus' ships, the Nina (meaning little girl), the Pinta (meaning painted lady), and the Santa Maria. Determine what sized square yields what sized boats. Form equations: if an 8.5" sq. makes a 4.5" boat, what size boat would a 6" sq. make *(analysis, synthesis)*?

4. Use the little boats to mark place settings, as nametags, necklaces, mobiles, or as part of a Columbus Day display or bulletin board *(application)*.

5. Experiment with different papers to find some that are actually waterproof. Choose various weights, textures, and fibers. Although somewhat more difficult to fold, include papers with foil backing or aluminum wrapping foil. Analyze the reasons why certain papers absorb water, and why others repel water. Spray absorbent papers with clear acrylic, paints, or other protective coatings. Evaluate the benefits of these types of sealants. Relate it to shipbuilding. Discuss the floatation and buoyancy of different materials and measure the saturation rates of boats made from different papers. Present the information on a chart that compares the various sinking times. Research the water-proofing methods used by shipbuilders in Columbus' time *(analysis, evaluation, synthesis)*.

6. Construct water-proof boats (use water-proof papers discovered in #5 or spray boats with a protective sealant) to test their stability in various wave and water conditions. Write down predictions or expectations before the experiments begin. Fill a broad basin alter-

nately with tap water, salt water, cold water, and hot water (or use several basins at the same time, set up as stations that the group can rotate between). Under each water condition, test for differences in sailing ability when the water is still or choppy. Observe and record results. Compare with initial expectations *(analysis, evaluation, synthesis)*.

7. Use Michael's ideas of what a flat world might be like to spur other thoughts about individual or group flat world fantasies. Use words to describe edge-of-the-world creatures and features, then illustrate with pictures. Present to the group or publish in a flat world handbook *(synthesis)*.

8. Research the British Flat Earth Society. Describe the rationale for its beliefs, despite photographs of the earth from outer space. Evaluate your own beliefs. Give several reasons why you agree or disagree with the Flat Earth Society. Present your beliefs in a persuasive format *(analysis, synthesis, evaluation)*.

9. Make a list of all the things that can be explored or discovered. Include diverse areas such as medicine, philosophy, biology, geography, earth science, space science, engineering, literature, or psychology. Be sure to include self-discovery as an area that requires no special equipment or training. Suggest methods of self-discovery, such as journal writing, values clarification, or the study of personal motivations and goals *(analysis, synthesis, evaluation)*.

10. Write your own stories about discovery or exploration. Illustrate with drawing, paper folding, or other methods. Work in small groups or individually. Present the results *(synthesis)*.

11. Sponsor a contest to see who can document the most places named for Columbus. Versions of his name include: Columbus, Colon, Colombo, Colom, and Colomb. Combine the results and display by making flags from paper and long pins, writing the locations on them, and sticking them into a large map to demonstrate the wide reaching appeal of his name *(analysis, synthesis)*.

Date	Group	Notes

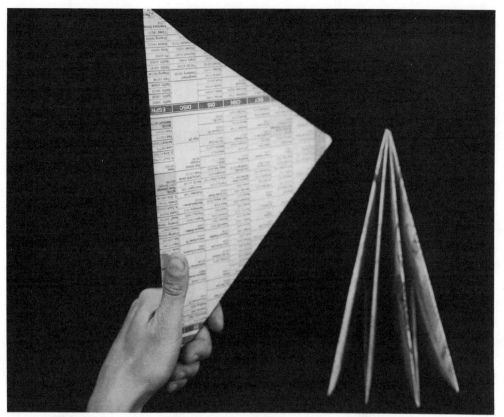

Flick the BOO! Machine and watch out! Folding directions begin on page 23.

About the story:

Last minute efforts to design a witch's hat lead to a surprising new Halloween invention.

Recommended ages: Listening only - age 3 through adult.
Listening and folding - age 7 through adult.

Required materials:

Start with one full sheet of newspaper that includes pictures or articles about Halloween events (usually 27 inches wide and 22 inches long), folded in half along its vertical midline. Fold it into a BOO! Machine, then completely unfold it for storytelling. <u>Note</u>: *This story should be delivered casually and conversationally (not read) as though you're simply telling your listeners about something that really happened to you that day. The surprise will be ruined if someone in the group has already heard the story, so it is most effective if presented only once to a particular group. It can be used as a humorous attention getter for warming up a group for other stories, or as a way to teach a simple origami noise-maker. You may wish to modify the text to adapt to your particular situation by adding the name of the city where you are speaking, changing the time of day, or adding details about yourself or the group you are addressing.*

GOTCHA!!

Before we actually get started with our Halloween activities today, I want to tell you a story about what happened to me this morning. I'd been planning for several weeks to teach you how to make a special Halloween craft, but with the school year starting and so many meetings to attend and fall activities to plan, I just never quite got around to making the final preparations. So this morning, there I sat reading this article in the morning paper *(hold up the newspaper)* about all the Halloween activities that are being offered around here. And then I got the most awful feeling that I had forgotten to do something. *(pause)* Oh no! It was your Halloween craft...I had forgotten to prepare your Halloween craft.

My first idea was to teach you how to fold a witch's hat that you could actually wear. So there I sat, looking at my newspaper, and I thought, why not make a newspaper witch's hat? I already had all the newspapers we would need, so I wouldn't have to go scurrying around for any more supplies. There was only one problem with this plan...I didn't know how to make a newspaper witch's hat. I was going to have to invent one.

The first thing I did was to find the center of this newspaper by folding it in half in both directions like this *(demonstrate with the preliminary fold)*.

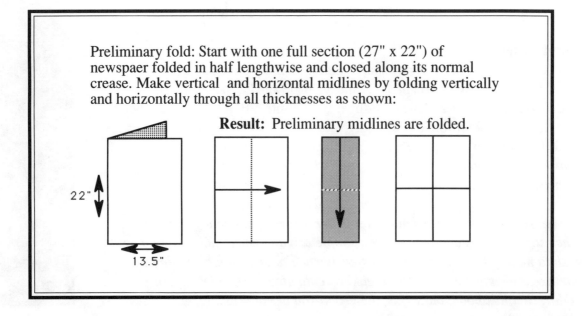

Preliminary fold: Start with one full section (27" x 22") of newspaer folded in half lengthwise and closed along its normal crease. Make vertical and horizontal midlines by folding vertically and horizontally through all thicknesses as shown:

Result: Preliminary midlines are folded.

22"

13.5"

What shape does a witch's hat have on top? *(Pause for someone to answer "pointed")*. Right! That's what I thought, too, so I folded the top corners down like this *(demonstrate with fold #1)*. Uh oh...this is not quite what we're looking for. We'd have to have heads six feet long to fit into this too-tall hat!

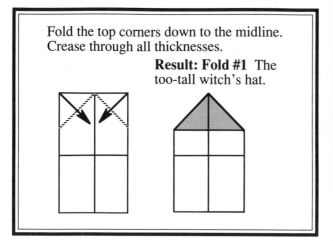

Fold the top corners down to the midline. Crease through all thicknesses.

Result: Fold #1 The too-tall witch's hat.

I thought that maybe I could make the hat shorter by folding the lower corners up like this *(demonstrate with fold #2)*. But this was even worse! Now I had a double-pointed arrow instead of a too-tall hat.

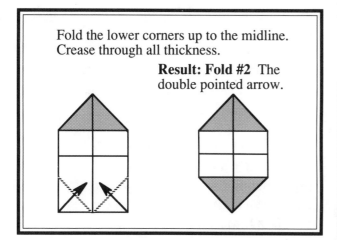

Fold the lower corners up to the midline. Crease through all thickness.

Result: Fold #2 The double pointed arrow.

I needed to get back to the pointed hat shape, so I decided to fold the double arrow in half like this *(demonstrate with fold #3)*. Now this is a better size and shape. *(Place the hat against your forehead)*. The only trouble is, with this fold in the bottom, it won't open to fit onto your head. So now I had a shorter witch's hat that couldn't be worn.

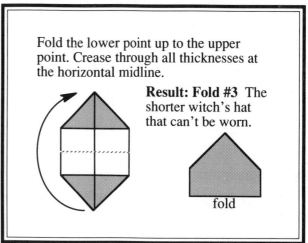

Fold the lower point up to the upper point. Crease through all thicknesses at the horizontal midline.

Result: Fold #3 The shorter witch's hat that can't be worn.

fold

By now, I was getting discouraged about making a witch's hat and I began to wonder what other Halloween symbol could be made out of this shape. Just as an experiment, I folded up the lower corners like this *(demonstrate with fold #4)*, checked to see that no one was watching, and zoomed this big-eared bat around my house. It was pretty fun, but somehow, a bat with no wings was not quite good enough for a group as sharp as you are.

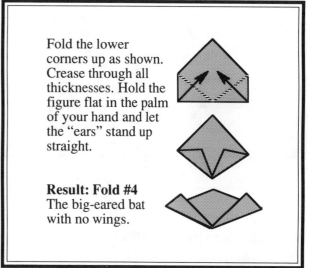

Fold the lower corners up as shown. Crease through all thicknesses. Hold the figure flat in the palm of your hand and let the "ears" stand up straight.

Result: Fold #4 The big-eared bat with no wings.

Although I could feel myself start to panic, all was not lost! I found out that if you get rid of these bat ears by unfolding them and then poking the corners to the inside, then you have little pockets *(demonstrate with fold #5)* that just might fit over your head.

Push the lower corners into the center of the model to form inside pockets. The corners will collapse inwards along the creases you made in fold #4.

Result: Fold #5 The witch's hat with inside pockets.

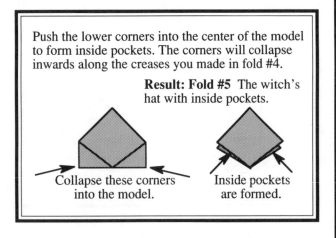

Collapse these corners into the model.

Inside pockets are formed.

(Try to fit your head into the pockets).

Well, I guess if you were a two-headed witch, this hat might work, but I don't see anyone in our group with two heads. I got to this point this morning and I thought I'd make one last try to find the proper hat shape. Whenever you fold the diamond in half like this *(demonstrate with fold #6)*, you always end up with a triangular shape.

Fold the outer points together and crease through all thickness at the vertical midline.

Result: Fold #6 The complete Boo! Machine.

Hold here.

Pockets

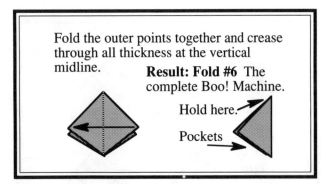

(Turn it upside down and examine it as you talk. Be sure to end up holding it where indicated in fold #6. You will know you're holding it correctly if the pockets are away from where your hand is squeezing the paper)

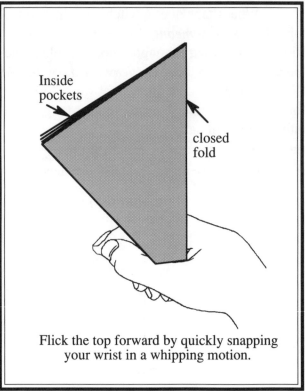

Flick the top forward by quickly snapping your wrist in a whipping motion.

Well, what do you think? It looks like a useless triangle to me. I was so frustrated this morning that I decided to just throw the whole thing away and start over from scratch! *(Flick the triangle down, filling the top pockets suddenly with air. A loud POP will result).*

Hey! What was that? *(Poke the folds back to the center and pop it again).*

It sounds like BOO! I know...a BOO! Machine. Who needs an old witch's hat when you can have a BOO! Machine? So after all that experimenting, we ended up with a terrific Halloween craft! Who would like to make their own BOO! Machine?

(Pop it again.) BOO!

Summary of folding directions:

Preliminary fold: Start with one full section (27" x 22") of newspaer folded in half lengthwise and closed along its normal crease. Make vertical and horizontal midlines by folding vertically and horizontally through all thicknesses as shown:

Result: Preliminary midlines are folded.

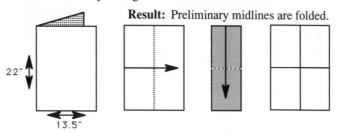

Fold the top corners down to the midline. Crease through all thicknesses.

Result: Fold #1 The too-tall witch's hat.

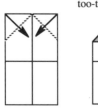

Fold the lower corners up to the midline. Crease through all thickness.

Result: Fold #2 The double pointed arrow.

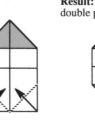

Fold the lower point up to the upper point. Crease through all thicknesses at the horizontal midline.

Result: Fold #3 The shorter witch's hat that can't be worn.

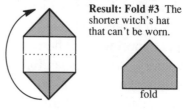

fold

Fold the lower corners up as shown. Crease through all thicknesses. Hold the figure flat in the palm of your hand and let the "ears" stand up straight.

Result: Fold #4 The big-eared bat with no wings.

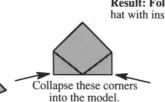

Push the lower corners into the center of the model to form inside pockets. The corners will collapse inwards along the creases you made in fold #4.

Result: Fold #5 The witch's hat with inside pockets.

Collapse these corners into the model.

Inside pockets are formed.

Fold the outer points together and crease through all thickness at the vertical midline.

Result: Fold #6 The complete Boo! Machine.

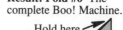

Hold here.

Pockets

HOLIDAY HISTORY

Why Things Go BOO! In October

The ghostly hauntings of Halloween spooks originated in the religious beliefs of three ancient cultures. Ancient Greeks believed that once a year, the souls of the dead returned to visit the earth. Rather than offend them, the Greeks held a week long festival, Anthesteria, where banquets were given in honor of the dead. When the week was over, the souls of the dead were sent back to the underworld by Greek priests who chanted, "Begone, ye ghosts: it is no longer Anthesteria."

The Roman festival Feralia was celebrated at the end of October. It was a religious day in Rome, dedicated to praying for the dead and honoring those heroes who had died for their country. Pre-Christian Romans celebrated another October holiday, the feast of Pomona, the goddess of orchards. They bobbed for apples and decorated their homes with fruits and nuts. They believed that protection from evil spirits could be achieved by hollowing out gourds and placing a lit candle or oil soaked rag inside.

In Druidism, the religion of the ancient Celtic people of Northern France and the British Isles, the last day of October, the feast of Summer's End or Samhain (pronounced *Sah'win*), marked the end of the growing and harvest season. November 1 was the beginning of winter and the new year. It was believed that during this time, the lord of death allowed the spirits of those who had died that year to return to earth for a few hours to warm themselves by the fireplace and to mingle with their families once again. Souls of the bad were condemned to enter the bodies of animals, while souls of the

good entered the body of another human being at death. Great bonfires were lit on hill tops to honor the Sun god and to frighten off evil spirits. Trick or treating began when groups of peasants went from house to house demanding food and money in the honor of Muck Olla (a lesser Druid god). Those who gave were assured of prosperity; those who didn't became victims of practical jokes and mischief. Celtic boys also went from house to house asking for sticks and logs for the great Samhain bonfires.

When the Romans conquered the Celtic lands and reigned there from 100 - 500 A. D., the rituals associated with the feast of Pomona were intermingled with the Druid rites. Uncomfortable with these pagan celebrations, Pope Gregory III designated November 1 as All Saints' or All Hallows' Day in the 8th century. By the Middle Ages, October 31 was known as All Hallows' E'en, and eventually was shortened to Halloween.

Halloween customs were introduced in America with the arrival of Irish and Scotch immigrants. Although the old-world superstitions and religious connections have disappeared in American Halloween celebrations, activities such as parading from house-to-house, bobbing for apples, eating fall fruits, and scaring each other with ghostly tales and haunted houses have continued to flourish. Although some fear that Halloween is historically linked to devil worship, the opposite is actually true. Traditional Halloween activities originated in efforts to *ward off* evil spirits, not to invite them in.

Optional applications for "Gotcha!"

1. After telling the story, listeners are usually very eager to make their own BOO! Machines. Review the problems encountered in trying to make the witch's hat. Identify each step by its story name: too-tall hat, double pointed arrow, short hat that can't be worn, etc. *(auditory sequential memory)*. Construct the model again, using a fresh, unfolded newspaper *(visual sequential memory)*. Ask the group to teach you each step, to reinforce their memories. When the group is confident that they understand how to construct the model, distribute sheets of newspaper for individual folding *(kinesthetic sequential memory)*. Fold together, step-by-step, or simply assist where needed *(synthesis)*.

2. Try using different newspapers, older and newer versions of the same newspaper, and various notebook or typing papers. Compare and contrast the popping volumes and how well different BOO! Machines hold up with repeated use. Do crisper papers make louder pops? Do older versions of the same brand of paper perform differently? Why are some papers softer than others? Which are the most effective and why? Demonstrate conclusions in group or individual presentations *(analysis, evaluation, synthesis)*.

3. Fold several BOO! Machines, all from different sized rectangles and various papers. Measure and record the decibels of each pop. Rank from loudest to softest. Select the loudest, the softest, and one from the middle. Ask participants to close their eyes and pop the selected BOO! Machines in random order; then ask each listener to write down his guess about the popping sequence. Compare results. Chart the number of correct responses with each trial. Repeat, using BOO! Machines with less distinct differences. Determine when the human ear is unable to discern volume differences. Do some listeners differentiate better than others? Propose possible explanations for individual hearing differences *(analysis, evaluation, synthesis)*.

4. Use the BOO! Machine as a rhythm instrument. Organize the group into a Boo band. Ask for volunteer conductors. Point to random BOO! Machines to be popped; pop up and down the rows in a controlled pulse; pop all of them simultaneously; count to 20 and pop only on numbers that start with certain letters (such as *N* or *T*), numbers that are divisible by a certain number, or on every 7th number.

5. Sing the song "Pop! Goes the Weasel". Play the BOO! Machine instead of singing the word "Pop". Put all but one of the BOO! Machines aside and form a circle. Choose a person to be the monkey who skips around the outside. Give the monkey the BOO! Machine. All sing, and when the "Pop" part occurs, the monkey pops his BOO! Machine behind a new monkey, trades places with him and gives him the BOO! Machine. Repeat until all players have a turn at being the monkey. If the group is large, divide into two or more circles and play simultaneously. If participants are inept at sticking the folds back into the BOO! Machine for repeated poppings, keep extra "loaded" ones on hand

to avoid delays. To maintain interest, vary the monkey's movements: hopping, skipping, tiptoeing, crawling, etc. or vary the way that the song is sung: volume, tempo, pitch, smoothness, etc. Halloween words can be substituted:

> "Round and round the haunted house,
> the witches chased the goblins,
> the witches thought it was all in fun,
> BOO! go the goblins!"

6. Sing "Skin and Bones" in a call and response style (the leader sings the verse and the group responds with the "Oo-oo" chorus). Instruct them to have "loaded" BOO! Machines ready. Challenge all group members to play simultaneously on the final "Boo!" Repeat with rhythm instruments that simulate footsteps, heart beats, a howling wind, owls hooting, or ghostly squeaks. Record and play back.

Skin and Bones - traditional Kentucky folk song

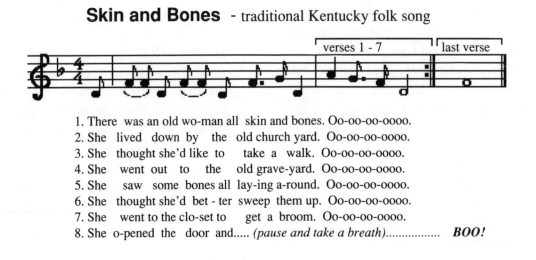

1. There was an old wo-man all skin and bones. Oo-oo-oo-oooo.
2. She lived down by the old church yard. Oo-oo-oo-oooo.
3. She thought she'd like to take a walk. Oo-oo-oo-oooo.
4. She went out to the old grave-yard. Oo-oo-oo-oooo.
5. She saw some bones all lay-ing a-round. Oo-oo-oo-oooo.
6. She thought she'd bet-ter sweep them up. Oo-oo-oo-oooo.
7. She went to the clo-set to get a broom. Oo-oo-oo-oooo.
8. She o-pened the door and..... *(pause and take a breath)*................ **BOO!**

Date	Group	Notes

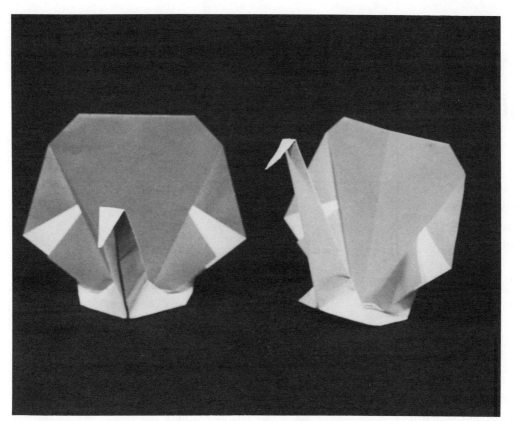

This cheerful turkey is made in seven easy steps. Folding directions begin on page 28.

About the story:

All the family members help with Thanksgiving preparations. They are rewarded with full stomachs and a satisfying sense of accomplishment.

Recommended ages: Listening only - age 3 through adult.
Listening and folding - age 5 through adult.

Required materials:

One square of paper at least six inches on each side, folded into a turkey and then completely unfolded for storytelling. Papers with different colored sides provide a sharp contrast for the tail feathers.

Optional introductory statement:

I'm going to tell you a story about how everyone in my family pitches in to help at Thanksgiving. Watch carefully as I fold this square (hold up the unfolded origami turkey) into various shapes. This is called origami, or Japanese paperfolding. The name of the story is "Helpgiving at Thanksgiving".

HELPGIVING AT THANKSGIVING

Helpgiving at Thanksgiving

Canadians substitute "cool October"

At my house in late November*,
When Thanksgiving time is near,
We always try to remember
That our help is mighty dear.

We all pitch in to help my mom
Who usually does the cooking.
She works hard to fix the feast
That's always so good looking.

Someone spreads the table cloth,
So clean and crisp and white,
And folds the napkins in half like this,
So the corners meet just right.
(Hold up fold #1).

We gather mums and pretty leaves
To make a fall bouquet,
(Hold up fold #2).
And find a vase with lots of water
To keep them fresh all day.
(Hold up fold #3).

We set the flowers in the center
As we sit and write our names.
(Make writing motions with fold #4).
Once a year place marks are set
For all the gents and dames.

Someone shines the gravy ladle,
Its top so smooth and round.
(Make ladling motions with fold #5).
Others set the formal table
With cheerful clinking sounds.

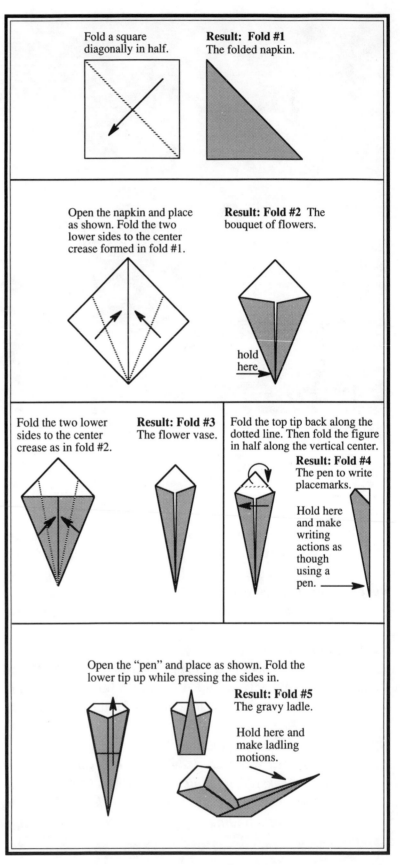

Fold a square diagonally in half.

Result: Fold #1 The folded napkin.

Open the napkin and place as shown. Fold the two lower sides to the center crease formed in fold #1.

Result: Fold #2 The bouquet of flowers.

hold here

Fold the two lower sides to the center crease as in fold #2.

Result: Fold #3 The flower vase.

Fold the top tip back along the dotted line. Then fold the figure in half along the vertical center.

Result: Fold #4 The pen to write placemarks.

Hold here and make writing actions as though using a pen.

Open the "pen" and place as shown. Fold the lower tip up while pressing the sides in.

Result: Fold #5 The gravy ladle.

Hold here and make ladling motions.

Now its time to scoop the food
Into the serving bowls,
(Make scooping motions with fold #6).
And place cranberry sauce
Next to the warm fresh rolls.

We light the candles and sing a hymn
Of praise and thanks sincere,
While quietly our stomachs say,
"Bring the turkey here!"

At last the youngest gives a shout,
"The turkey! It is done!"
Mom brings the bird right on out
For Thanksgiving dinner fun.
(Hold up fold #7).

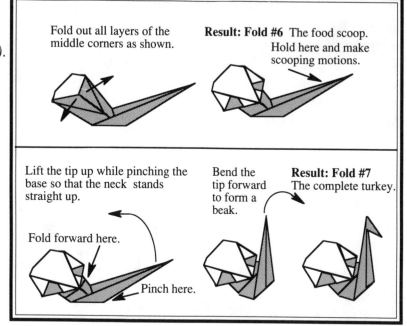

Fold out all layers of the middle corners as shown.

Result: Fold #6 The food scoop. Hold here and make scooping motions.

Lift the tip up while pinching the base so that the neck stands straight up.

Fold forward here.

Pinch here.

Bend the tip forward to form a beak.

Result: Fold #7 The complete turkey.

HOLIDAY HISTORY

Why turkey at Thanksgiving?

In the autumn of 1621, Plymouth Colony Governor William Bradford declared three days of feasting and thanksgiving to celebrate the Pilgrims' first bountiful harvest in the New World. To prepare for the feast, the Pilgrim men went "fowling", presumably hunting for ducks, geese, partridge, and turkeys. There is no written account, however, that turkeys were actually eaten at that first Thanksgiving feast. All that was documented in journals was that deer, duck, geese, seafood, cornbread, leeks, watercress, greens, wild plums, dried berries, plain boiled pumpkins, and hasty pudding (boiled corn) were on the menu. Because the Pilgrims were without cows, there were no dairy products. Wheat was not successfully cultivated for many years to come, so there was no crust for pumpkin pie.

Although many special days of thanksgiving had been declared by various state gover-

nors, continental congresses, and United States presidents, Thanksgiving did not become an annual event until 1863, when President Lincoln issued the first national Thanksgiving Proclamation, setting the last Thursday in November as the day to be observed. Mrs. Josepha Hale, the editor of *Godey's Lady's Book*, began a relentless letter writing campaign in 1827, appealing for a uniform day of national thanks. Her last editorial on the subject, printed 36 years later in September 1863, contained her most persuasive arguments. A Congressional Joint Resolution approved by President Franklin D. Roosevelt in 1941 officially designated the fourth Thursday in November as Thanksgiving Day throughout the country.

Turkey did not become customary Thanksgiving fare until the early nineteenth century, and was not the traditional main course until the 1860's. After World War II, the poultry industry conducted an aggressive marketing campaign to further entrench the concept of Thanksgiving turkey. This effort coincided with the development of hybrid birds and helped to promote the stuffed gobbler as a symbol of American abundance.

Thanksgiving itself stems from ancient harvest festival traditions prevalent in almost every agricultural society. The most direct connection is with the Pilgrims, who performed Harvest Home ceremonies at various intervals throughout the calendar.

Optional applications for "*Help*giving at Thanksgiving"

1. After reciting the poem, ask the listeners to identify, in order, the Thanksgiving help that was given *(auditory sequential memory)*. Construct the turkey again, using a fresh unfolded square of paper *(visual sequential memory)*. Be sure to use the correct names for each step: the folded napkins, the flower bouquet, the vase, etc. so that the paired associations are reinforced. When the group is confident about the folding sequence, distribute squares of paper for individual folding *(kinesthetic memory)*. Fold together, step-by-step, or assist only when necessary. Distribute smaller and smaller squares to increase confidence, memory, and precision.

2. Decorate the finished turkey by drawing feathers and facial features. Ask the group to visualize where the markings would occur on a flat, unfolded square, and then draw those markings on another, unfolded square of paper. Unfold the decorated square and compare it to the flat paper to judge the accuracy of the predictions. Build the turkey from the flat paper to demonstrate where their predictions really ended up *(analysis)*. Repeat. Did the predictions improve on the second trial?

3. Compose a new version of the poem from the group's helping suggestions. Merely substitute the new ideas, or develop an entirely new structure. Think of other things the folds could represent *(synthesis)*.

4. Use the origami turkeys as nametags, necklaces or earrings, as part of a mobile or bulletin board display, or as a Thanksgiving card, with a message written on the tail *(application)*.

5. Construct a large turkey from a grocery bag, or other large sheet of sturdy paper (at least 14" per side). Place a basket of fruit or flowers between the tail and neck to form a centerpiece. Decorate the tail with post-it-notes containing ideas for helping in your group setting, such as picking up left-over supplies, helping each other carry heavy loads, being good listeners, etc. Write the suggestions yourself, or ask each group member to contribute ideas. Complete the activity by asking each group member to take a turn in randomly selecting a feather and then without words, pantomiming the helpful idea until the others guess what it is. Challenge the group to continue helping in that

way for the rest of the day. Share the fruit and flowers after a successful day of helping each other *(application, synthesis, evaluation)*.

6. Use the poem as part of a Thanksgiving pageant or presentation. Choose a narrator, or have all students recite together. Construct a giant turkey from a very large sheet of paper, with one or two different people assigned to each step. Make sure that all group members contribute in some way, demonstrating the spirit of cooperation and helping each other *(application, synthesis)*.

7. Research the history and/or trends of turkey consumption and production. Invite a guest speaker from the poultry industry or a meat market to speak and bring samples of various turkey products. Follow up with written summaries, humorous pictures of "turkey-dogs", or discussions evaluating issues of taste, nutrition, or economic influences *(analysis, synthesis, evaluation)*.

8. Discuss the feelings associated with taking responsibility or in offering assistance. When is self-concept at its highest? Lowest? How do the concepts of self-concept and responsibility interact *(analysis, evaluation)*?

9. Sponsor a turkey day fun fest with relay races or an obstacle course featuring a turkey walk, turkey gobble, turkey balance, or turkey toss. Use the origami turkeys in these events. Compare to the contests featured at the Pilgrim's first Thanksgiving with the local Indians *(application, synthesis)*.

Date	Group	Notes

This dreidel was constructed out of an 11 inch square of computer paper. See page 10 for hints about how to make squares from rectangular papers. The handle can be a tightly rolled piece of paper as shown here, or simply a straw, pencil, or narrow piece of wooden dowel. Directions for three different versions of dreidel games begin on page 38. A dreidel song and dance can be found on page 39.

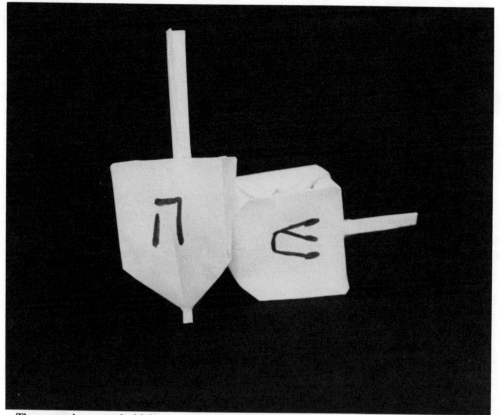

These sturdy paper dreidels are a variation of the traditional origami water bomb. Folding directions begin on page 37.

About the story:

Judah Maccabee leads a rebellion against the Syrian King, Antiochus, in order to save the Jewish religion from further destruction. When he emerges victorious and rededicates the temple in Jerusalem, a short supply of oil lasts for a miraculously long time.

Recommended ages: Listening only - age 5 through adult.
                                    Listening and folding - age 7 through adult.

Required materials:

A marking pen; a pencil, straw, or tightly rolled paper to insert as the dreidel handle; and one square of sturdy paper at least 8 inches on each side, folded through step #4 and then completely unfolded for storytelling.

Optional introductory statement:

I'm going to tell you a story about how a small group of brave people fought back against a terrible king. Watch carefully as I fold this square (hold up the unfolded origami dreidel) into various shapes. This is called origami, or Japanese paperfolding. The name of the story is "A Miracle Happened There".

A Miracle Happened There

2,000 years ago, the world was very different than it is today. People lived for most of their lives in small areas, without relocating or moving about as we do now. Most had no knowledge of written language or communication, and radio and television were many centuries away from being invented. So all that the people knew, came from their own personal experiences or from stories or information shared by others that lived around them. When travelers passed through, they were regarded with both suspicion and great interest. The most dramatic changes occurred when foreign armies conquered new territories. They brought with them new ideas and new traditions. In some cases, the conquerors made it illegal to practice the old, comfortable traditions, and forced their ways on people who didn't want to change.

We can think of the old world as being divided into smaller areas that were controlled by powerful 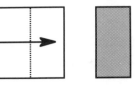 rulers with powerful armies. *(Fold a square in half and point to each half, as though the halves represent sections of the world)* .

For example, in the Middle East, the Greeks had been in control for many years, but then the Romans began to challenge them. *(Fold the resulting rectangle in half, and*

point to the top section to represent the Greeks and the lower section to represent the Romans).

Caught in the middle between their struggles were other smaller groups of people *(Fold the smaller square into a triangle to represent the smaller groups),* including the Jews who had to pay taxes to the Greeks and obey Greek rules, but were basically allowed to practice their own Jewish religion without too much interference.

There was no interference, that is, until a Syrian King named Antiochus IV came into power. He sent his armies to Jerusalem with orders to destroy the Jewish religion and replace it with his own religion. Because he believed in a god named Zeus, he thought that everyone should believe in Zeus too. He wanted everyone in the world to pray the same way that he prayed. So his armies marched in and tore down the Jewish altars, made it illegal to be Jewish, and put up statues of Zeus in the temples. If Jewish people refused to follow these orders, they were punished in terrible ways.

The people were afraid and outnumbered by the armies of Antiochus IV, so it wasn't until the army came to destroy this temple *(hold up fold #1)* in a little village named Modi'in, that the Jewish people began to fight back.

The army troops wanted to squash the Jewish religion like this *(demonstrate with the first corner of fold #2)* but instead, Mattathias, a Jewish leader in the village of Modi'in, squashed the troops like this *(demonstrate with the second corner of fold #2).*

Knowing that he and his family would be in big trouble for refusing to give up their Jewish religion, Mattathias and his sons headed up to the hills *(point to a place on the triangle formed in fold #2)*, where they were soon joined by other Jews who were willing to fight to save the temples. Mattathias died during one of the battles, but his son, Judah, who was called Maccabee, or hammerer, assumed leadership of the rebellion. The fighters became known as the Maccabees and as their numbers grew, so did the numbers of battles.

(Begin folding Fold #3 as you say the number years passing by. Fold one corner up for each time period). The battles were fought for *six months, one year, two years*, and finally, at the end of *three years*, the Maccabees reclaimed the temple in Jerusalem, the first temple that was damaged by Antiochus.

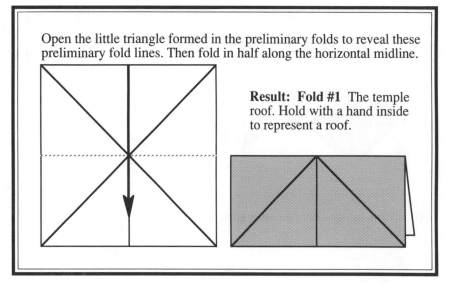

Open the little triangle formed in the preliminary folds to reveal these preliminary fold lines. Then fold in half along the horizontal midline.

Result: Fold #1 The temple roof. Hold with a hand inside to represent a roof.

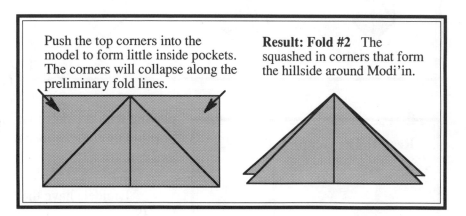

Push the top corners into the model to form little inside pockets. The corners will collapse along the preliminary fold lines.

Result: Fold #2 The squashed in corners that form the hillside around Modi'in.

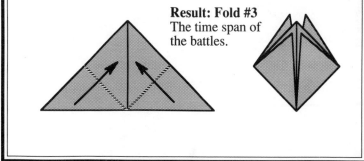

Fold the lower corners up to the top on the front side. Then repeat on the flip side. Say: "*6 months*", "*one year*", "*two years*", and "*three years*" as you fold each corner up.

Result: Fold #3 The time span of the battles.

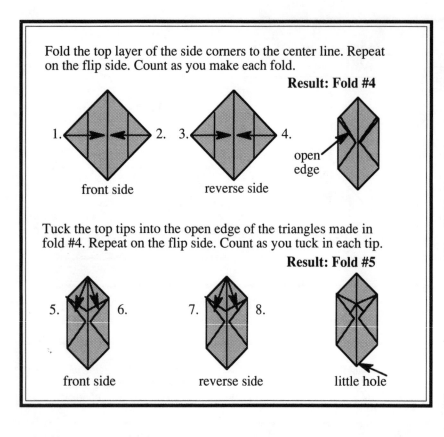

Fold the top layer of the side corners to the center line. Repeat on the flip side. Count as you make each fold.

Result: Fold #4

open edge

front side

reverse side

Tuck the top tips into the open edge of the triangles made in fold #4. Repeat on the flip side. Count as you tuck in each tip.

Result: Fold #5

front side

reverse side

little hole

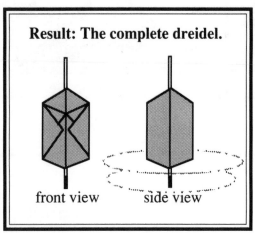

Result: The complete dreidel.

front view

side view

Judah and his brothers declared that the rededication of the temple should be celebrated for eight days that year, the first Hanukkah, and for eight days in every future year, too. They brought in a candlestick to light the lamps. There was only enough oil to keep them burning for one day, but miraculously, the lamps kept ablaze for one, two, three, four, five, six, seven, all eight days. *(Fold a part of folds #4 and #5 as you rhythmically count each number).*

And that is why Jewish children breathe fun *(inflate the figure through the little hole on the bottom of the model)* into Hanukkah celebrations by playing with dreidels that look like this. *(Insert a pencil or a tightly rolled paper rod through the inflated figure and spin it).*

Dreidels have the Hebrew symbols for the letters NGHS *(write the symbols or words on each side)* which stand for, *Nes gadol hayah sham*, "A great miracle happened there".

Nun *(nothing)*   Gimel *(all)*   Heh *(half)*   Shin *(put in)*

Summary of folding directions:

Preliminary creases:

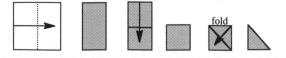

Open the little triangle formed in the preliminary folds to reveal these preliminary fold lines. Then fold in half along the horizontal midline.

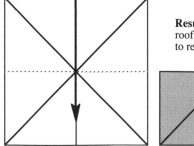

Result: Fold #1 The temple roof. Hold with a hand inside to represent a roof.

Push the top corners into the model to form little inside pockets. The corners will collapse along the preliminary fold lines.

Result: Fold #2 The squashed in corners that form the hillside around Modi'in.

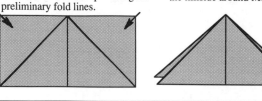

Fold the lower corners up to the top on the front side. Then repeat on the flip side. Say: *"6 months"*, *"one year"*, *"two years"*, and *"three years"* as you fold each corner up.

Result: Fold #3 The time span of the battles.

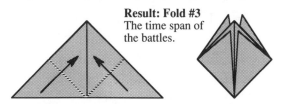

Fold the top layer of the side corners to the center line. Repeat on the flip side. Count as you make each fold.

Result: Fold #4

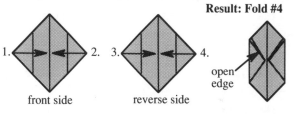

1. 2. 3. 4. open edge

front side   reverse side

Tuck the top tips into the open edge of the triangles made in fold #4. Repeat on the flip side. Count as you tuck in each tip.

Result: Fold #5

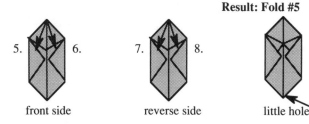

5. 6. 7. 8.

front side   reverse side   little hole

Inflate the dreidel through the little hole. Insert a pencil or a tightly rolled paper rod to spin.

Result: The complete dreidel.

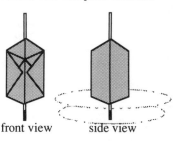

front view   side view

HOLIDAY HISTORY — Where did the *dreidel originate?

Although the dreidel is often considered as *the* protypical Jewish toy, it is simply a variation of the spinning top that was introduced to Japan from China and Korea over 1,200 years ago. Enjoyed first by Japanese aristocrats, the spinning tops later spread to the common people.

"Quarreling tops" were popular in Japan, and were used in gambling. It is possible that the Jewish dreidels descended from the spindle-whorl used for spinning thread in ancient Japan. Jews often adapted games found in their sur-

*also spelled dreidl or dreydl

rounding culture to their own needs. Some scholars believe that dreidel playing was used to disguise Jewish prayer meetings in times of persecution. Historians speculate that game playing may have begun during the Maccabean struggle. It is well documented that the modern four-sided dreidel was a common **Hanukkah game among Ashkenazic Jews at the beginning of the Middle Ages.

In Israel, dreidels are made with the letter *pe* instead of *shin*, signifying that "a great miracle happened *here*". Dreidels have been made out of diverse materials, including silver, ivory, wood, clay, and paper mache. It is interesting that the dreidel in this story is folded from paper; an ancient Japanese top made through ancient Japanese paper folding techniques.

**also spelled Chanukkah, Chanukah, Hanukah, Hannukah

Dreidel Games

The dreidel game is played by spinning the top around and waiting to see which figure turns up. Nun means nothing, gimel means all, heh means half, and shin means put. Every player puts the same amount of candy, nuts, or chips into the kitty, spins the dreidel, then pays the penalty: nun, nothing happens; gimel, the player wins the pot; heh, the player gets half of what's in the kitty; and shin, the player must contribute whatever has been agreed upon to the kitty.

Another version of the game assigns numerical values to the symbols: Nun = 50, Gimel = 3, Heh = 5, Shin = 300. The players agree beforehand upon a goal. They keep track of their points and the first one to reach the goal, is the winner.

A third way to play with the dreidel involves spinning skill. A record is kept of the length of the actual spinning time. The player who can spin the dreidel for the longest time within a predetermined number of tries is the winner. It is usually required that the dreidel remain within a given area, such as a table top, or within a circle.

*Dreydl Dance

Set up: Dancers arrange themselves in a circle, hands joined and facing the center. One dancer, placed in the middle, is the Dreydl.

part 1: Dancers in the circle walk around clockwise, taking 16 steps, singing the first part of the song, "I Have A Little Dreydl", stopping when the "O dreydl" chorus begins. Meanwhile, the dreydl in the center, turns in place. On the last few counts, the dreydl chooses a partner and pulls him into the center.

part 2: This part begins with the "O dreydl" chorus. The circle dancers stand and clap hands 16 times while the two inside the circle whirl each other around, either with hooked arms, or with both hands held, facing each other. On the last few counts, the dancer who was the original dreydl joins the outer circle while the chosen dancer remains in the center for the next verse. For large groups or if available time is restricted, both dancers join the outer circle. The new dreydl is selected by the dancer who was chosen by the first dreydl.

The song is repeated until all dancers have a turn.

*adapted from a circle game by Dvora Lapson

I Have a Little Dreydl

by Samuel S. Grossman & Samuel E. Goldfarb

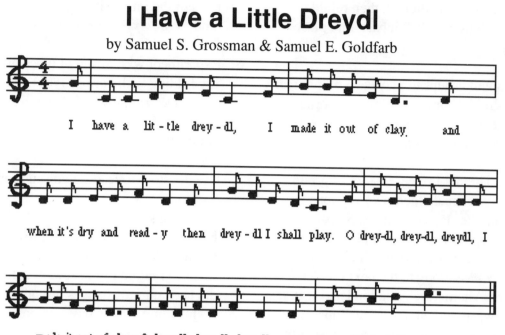

I have a lit-tle drey-dl, I made it out of clay. and
when it's dry and read-y then drey-dl I shall play. O drey-dl, drey-dl, drey-dl, I
made it out of clay; O drey-dl, drey-dl, drey-dl, now drey-dl I shall play.

2. It has a lovely body with leg so short and thin; and
   when it is all tired, it drops and then I win. O dreydl, dreydl, dreydl, with
   leg so short and thin; O dreydl, dreydl, dreydl, it drops and then I win.

3. My dreydl, always playful, it loves to dance and spin; a
   happy game of dreydl; Come play, now let's begin. O dreydl, dreydl, dreydl, it
   loves to dance and spin; O dreydl, dreydl, dreydl, come play, now let's begin.

Optional applications for "A Miracle Happened There"

1. After telling the story, review the steps necessary to fold the dreidel, using the names from the story: the temple roof, the squashed temple, the hillside, etc. *(auditory sequential memory)*. Next, construct the dreidel again with a fresh, unfolded piece of paper, asking the group to tell you what step comes next *(visual sequential memory)*. Point out the importance of lining up the edges before forming the creases. When the group is confident that they know the folding sequence, distribute squares of paper. Fold together, step-by-step, or encourage individual folding, depending on the ability and age of the group *(kinesthetic sequential memory)*.

2. Write the Hebrew symbols on the sides. Predict where they will fall on the unfolded paper. Unfold the dreidel, then refold to observe the symbols fall back into place *(analysis)*.

3. Form small groups to play each of the traditional dreidel games. Choose a favorite. Evaluate the reasons why it is the favorite *(application, evaluation)*.

4. Try the Dreidel Dance. Challenge group members to create their own versions by changing the steps or actions. Substitute rhythm instruments for clapping. Drape a flowing scarf on the inside dreidel dancers that they pass along to the next dreidel dancers. Alternate singing loud and soft, fast and slow, smooth and choppy. Tape record or video tape for later viewing. Present in a Hanukkah celebration or demonstration *(application, synthesis)*.

5. Research the origin of tops as toys. Compare and contrast tops from different cultures. Present the information with illustrations or models *(analysis, synthesis)*.

6. Experiment with different types of handles. Try folding with various types and weights of paper. Determine which combination spins the most effectively *(analysis, evaluation, synthesis)*.

7. Use the story to lead into discussions or units about:
   a. Hanukkah traditions.
   b. Historical significance of toys.
   c. Significance for other religions of the preservation of the Jewish culture.
   d. The cultural changes brought about by invading armies past and present.
   e. Courage required to maintain values despite danger and humiliation.

Date	Group	Notes

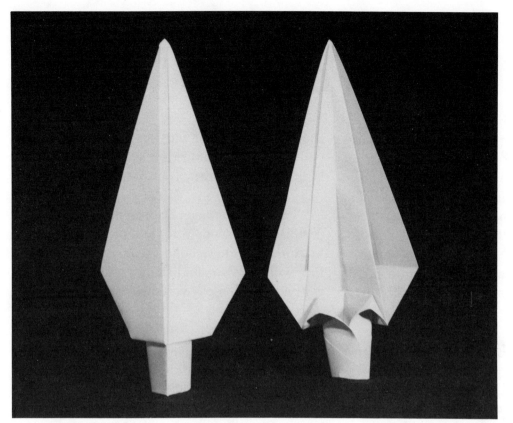

Folding directions for this elegant free-standing tree are on page 46. Front and back views are shown here.

About the story:

After his uncle suffers a bad fall at Oktoberfest, Martin Ritter leaves home to help him prepare his farm for the harsh Wisconsin winter. His parents are sorry to see Martin go, but he promises to be home in time to light the Christbaum with his family.

Recommended ages: Listening only - age 3 through adult.
Listening and folding - age 5 through adult.

Required materials:

One square of paper at least six inches on each side, folded into a tree and then completely unfolded for storytelling.

Optional introductory statement:

I'm going to tell you a story about a German boy named Martin, who lived in Wisconsin over 100 years ago. Watch carefully as I fold this square (hold up the unfolded origami tree) into various shapes. This is called origami, or Japanese paperfolding. The name of the story is "Home for Christmas".

Home For Christmas

Indian summer in Central Wisconsin had arrived just in time for the 1880 Oktoberfest. All the German families in the county came to the three day festival, raising Herr Gottmich's barn by day, and dancing and eating by night. The harvest had been rich this summer and none of the German families feared the coming winter months like they had last year when drought killed the corn and even the milk cows had to be slaughtered.

Only one problem marred the otherwise perfect festivities. Martin Ritter's Uncle Hermann broke his leg in a fall from the roof of the new barn. "Too much bratwurst and sauerkraut for lunch," claimed Aunt Elsa. "He was lucky not to have crushed his neck with the weight of all that food crashing down on it."

"Who will do your milking, Uncle Hermann?" asked Martin, who was 16 and already taller than any of the other men in the family. "Who will get your farm ready for winter?"

"Have you been reading my mind, nephew?"

"Nein, Uncle, but I heard Herr Schmidt say that you should not move about for at least two weeks, and then after that, only a little at a time until Christmas comes."

"Jah, my healed leg will be the best Christmas gift I've ever gotten."

"I've been thinking. Otto is thirteen now and finished his schooling last year. He's strong enough to help Vater with our farm. I will help you with yours until Christmas time. That will keep the bankers away from your land."

Uncle Hermann clapped the broad shouldered Martin. "Your Vater will be proud of you, Martin. I don't have dollars to pay you, but my Elsa will make you fat like me. And don't you worry. We will repay you some time when you least expect it."

And so it was that Martin Ritter drove his uncle's family home after the Oktoberfest of 1880. "I will light the top candle of the Christbaum," Martin promised his proud, but teary mother. "I will see you at Christmas."

As expected, the weather turned windy and cold before the end of October. Aunt Elsa's hands never rested as she rushed to put up the last fall vegetables and apples. Martin dug, while his little cousins followed behind, stooping over to gather the last potatoes, beets, and carrots from the garden. He chopped wood for the winter, and fed and milked the dairy cows. Once a week, Martin delivered cheese to the corner trading post where the train stopped to bring it to the markets in Madison. Exhausted every night, Martin hardly had time to think about missing his parents and his brothers.

Uncle Hermann issued orders, but there wasn't much he could actually do. So he sat by the fire and carved figurines modeled after the twirling folk dancers and musicians from the old country in Bavaria. They would be Christmas gifts for Martin's family.

In the first week of December, the lakes froze and a deep snow blanketed all of Central Wisconsin like this *(use the unfolded square of paper to demonstrate a blanketing effect)*. Now when Martin went out to the barn, he covered his head and shoulders with a large wool scarf that looked like this *(demonstrate with fold #1)*:

As Christmas grew closer, Uncle Hermann's leg became stronger and he put more weight on it every day. Early on the morning of December 24, Martin was chiseling chunks of ice to melt for the animals with a sharp tool that looked like this *(demonstrate with fold #2)*:

"It is time for you to go home to light the Christbaum with your family," said Uncle Hermann. "Look at the skies. We must leave now. I fear more snow will come, and if the drifts build up, the horses may not get through. Go now and get your things while I hitch the team."

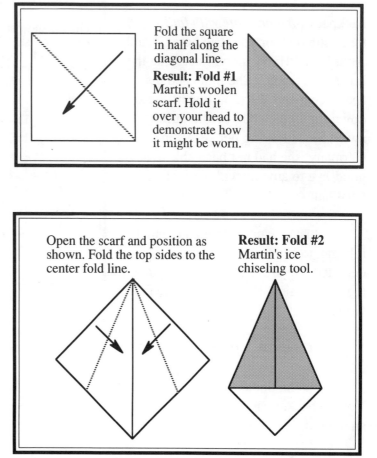

Fold the square in half along the diagonal line.
Result: Fold #1 Martin's woolen scarf. Hold it over your head to demonstrate how it might be worn.

Open the scarf and position as shown. Fold the top sides to the center fold line.
Result: Fold #2 Martin's ice chiseling tool.

Aunt Elsa packed with quick, deft hands. "Take these new snowshoes Uncle Hermann made for you," she said. *(Hold up fold #3.)* She pressed them into his hands and dashed away to the pantry to hide her good-bye tears.

She returned with jars of wild strawberry preserves and apple jelly. A salted ham, wooden figurines and toys, fresh cheese, and strips of dried beef were already packed.

"Put these jellies into this new

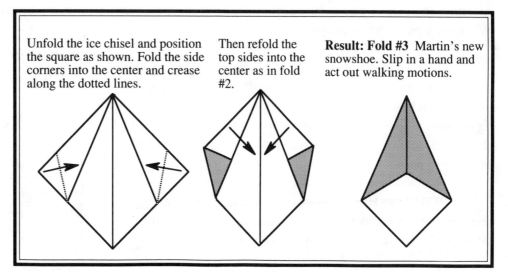

Unfold the ice chisel and position the square as shown. Fold the side corners into the center and crease along the dotted lines.

Then refold the top sides into the center as in fold #2.

Result: Fold #3 Martin's new snowshoe. Slip in a hand and act out walking motions.

backpack *(demonstrate with fold #4)* that I stitched for your trip home," said Aunt Elsa. "Hurry, now. I hear that the horses are ready." She tightened his heavy coat and scarf, pulling his head down for a quick hug before turning away. Since leaving her sisters in Germany, she had not been able to say good-bye to anyone without feeling very sad.

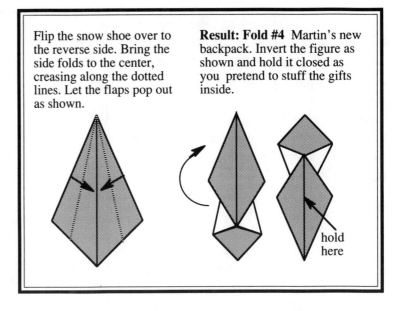

Flip the snow shoe over to the reverse side. Bring the side folds to the center, creasing along the dotted lines. Let the flaps pop out as shown.

Result: Fold #4 Martin's new backpack. Invert the figure as shown and hold it closed as you pretend to stuff the gifts inside.

hold here

Just as Uncle Hermann feared, it began to snow shortly after they departed. He drove the sleigh as far as the train station, but then the snowfall worsened.

"Come back home with me, Martin. My brother will understand."

"Nein, uncle. I promised Vater und Muter I'd be home for the lighting of the Christbaum. You go back. I can walk the rest of the way on the new snowshoes you made for me. It's only another eight miles and I know the way well. Aunt Elsa sent plenty of food."

"The night comes early, Martin. Make haste. And don't forget my promise. One day we will repay your kindness."

Martin strapped on his backpack and new snowshoes. His clothes were several layers thick, and although it was snowing harder than ever, the wind was not harsh and the temperature did not seem to be getting colder. The large, wet flakes covered the ground in a deep layer of sticky white. Martin's snowshoes packed it down, his long stride steady and strong, his breathing sure and regular. Walk walk puff walk walk puff....

After a couple miles, Martin leaned against a birch tree to rest and eat his lunch of cheese and dried beef. The hardwoods stretched out their naked branches, letting the snow slip right through their slender fingers, while the evergreens bowed their heads and opened their arms, welcoming even heavier burdens of snow.

"Hoo Hoo Hoo ha Hoooooo," came a cry echoing through the woods. A wood owl *(demonstrate with fold #5)* as white as the snow swooped down and landed above him.

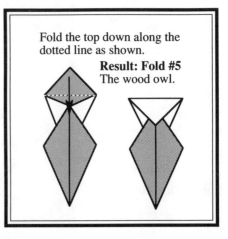

Fold the top down along the dotted line as shown.

Result: Fold #5 The wood owl.

"Are you an angel from heaven, friend owl?" whispered Martin. "Guide me home, and you can roost on the tip top of the Christbaum."

But the snowy bird just closed its eyes, hunched up its shoulders and buried its beak into its fluffy chest like this *(demonstrate with fold #6).*

The owl must have brought him good luck, for shortly after Martin paused to eat, it stopped snowing and the clouds

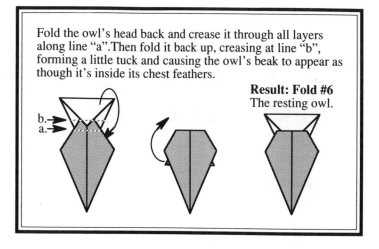

Fold the owl's head back and crease it through all layers along line "a". Then fold it back up, creasing at line "b", forming a little tuck and causing the owl's beak to appear as though it's inside its chest feathers.

Result: Fold #6
The resting owl.

began to break up. Although the day's light was almost gone, the freshly fallen snow gave the woods an eerie brightness. Soon, the first glimmer of starlight appeared and the moon rose above the trees. Walking as quickly as possible, Martin was almost to the little frozen creek that marked the outer edges of his family's farm.

He swung his snowshoes out and around with renewed vigor, pausing only when he smelled the friendly smoke of his family's hearth. He pulled off his cap and leaned his ear toward the sweet music that drifted across the meadow.

"Stile Nacht, Heilige Nacht!"

He rushed forward as the lights of the Christbaum began to twinkle, there out in the farm-yard, their cows and horses looking on as the family lit the candles, one by one.

"I'm home!" he shouted. "I'm home for Christmas!"

All smiles, amid hugs and holiday kisses, Martin lit the last candle, just as he had promised he would. *(Point to the top of fold #7).* Yes, it was good to be home. It was good to be home for Christmas.

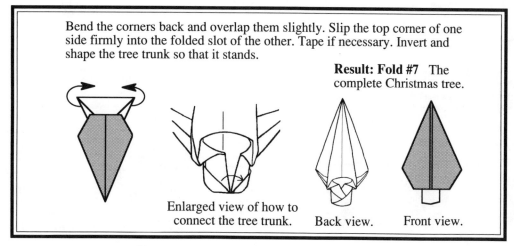

Bend the corners back and overlap them slightly. Slip the top corner of one side firmly into the folded slot of the other. Tape if necessary. Invert and shape the tree trunk so that it stands.

Result: Fold #7 The complete Christmas tree.

Enlarged view of how to connect the tree trunk.

Back view.

Front view.

Summary of folding directions:

Fold the square in half along the diagonal line.
Result: Fold #1 Martin's woolen scarf. Hold it over your head to demonstrate how it might be worn.

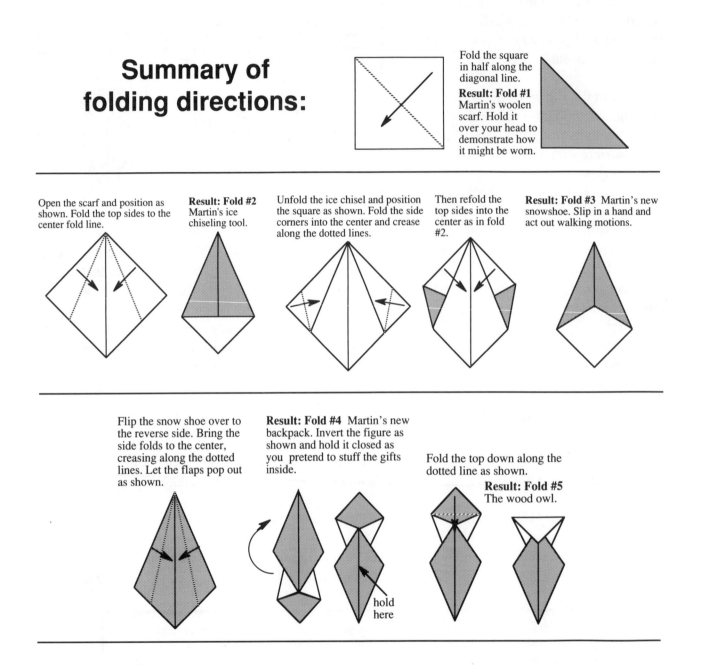

Open the scarf and position as shown. Fold the top sides to the center fold line.

Result: Fold #2 Martin's ice chiseling tool.

Unfold the ice chisel and position the square as shown. Fold the side corners into the center and crease along the dotted lines.

Then refold the top sides into the center as in fold #2.

Result: Fold #3 Martin's new snowshoe. Slip in a hand and act out walking motions.

Flip the snow shoe over to the reverse side. Bring the side folds to the center, creasing along the dotted lines. Let the flaps pop out as shown.

Result: Fold #4 Martin's new backpack. Invert the figure as shown and hold it closed as you pretend to stuff the gifts inside.

Fold the top down along the dotted line as shown.

Result: Fold #5 The wood owl.

hold here

Fold the owl's head back and crease it through all layers along line "a". Then fold it back up, creasing at line "b", forming a little tuck and causing the owl's beak to appear as though it's inside its chest feathers.

Result: Fold #6 The resting owl.

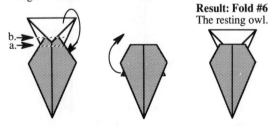

b.—
a.—

Bend the corners back and overlap them slightly. Slip the top corner of one side firmly into the folded slot of the other. Tape if necessary. Invert and shape the tree trunk so that it stands.

Result: Fold #7 The complete Christmas tree.

Enlarged view of how to connect the tree trunk.

Back view. Front view.

HOLIDAY HISTORY

Why a tree at Christmas?

Several legends attempt to explain why evergreen trees have become such a popular and important symbol of the Christmas season. A favorite one asserts that Ansgarius, an early Christian, was sent among the Vikings of the North to preach Christianity. Three messengers, Faith, Hope, and Love, were sent with him to find and light the first Christmas tree. They sought one that was as high as hope, as wide as love, and had the sign of the cross (faith) on every bough. The balsam fir seemed to meet these requirements and was chosen.

It is also widely reported that Martin Luther wandered through the woods one starry Christmas Eve and became enamored of the wonders of the night. He cut a small snowy fir tree, returned home, and set it up for his children. He illuminated it with candles to represent the beautiful stars he had just enjoyed in the forest.

Another legend describes how in the eighth century, St. Boniface persuaded the Teutons to give up their cruel practice of sacrificing a child before a great oak tree during their midwinter festival. Instead, he said, "Cut down a big fir tree, take it home, and celebrate around it with your innocent children." He told them that fir was the wood of peace from which their houses were built and the sign of immortality, since its leaves were ever green and its top branches pointed straight to heaven.

The most likely start of the evergreen Christmas tradition occurred in the fourteenth and fifteenth centuries when the designated miracle play for December 24 was the story of Adam and Eve. The chief prop was an apple hung evergreen called the paradise tree. This may have led directly to German families bringing evergreens into their homes during the holiday season, believed to have begun in the sixteenth century.

By the next century, these were known as Christbaume (Christ trees) and were decorated with fruit, candies, cookies, and cut wafers. Candles were also introduced during this period. The Christmas tree tradition remained German until it was introduced in England by German merchants in the nineteenth century and popularized by Prince Albert of Saxe-Coburg.

Many believe that Christmas trees were first introduced to America by the Hessian Germans sent by the English to fight in the American Revolution. They were later set up by German immigrants in Pennsylvania in the 1820's. Wherever the Christmas-keeping Germans went, there also appeared Christmas trees. In the remote pioneer cabins, toys were handmade and decorations were constructed from materials gathered in the woods and fields. New mittens, corn husk dolls, gingerbread cookies, and simple ribbon bows adorned the evergreens.

Universal adoption of the custom was not established until 1910. The first public American Christmas tree was decorated with lights and tinsel in Pasadena, California, in 1909. A tall evergreen on Mount Wilson was selected and loaded with gifts that were distributed on Christmas Day. The first trees were set up in Madison Square in New York and on the Common in Boston in 1912, and Philadelphia began its Christmas tree tradition in 1914. President Calvin Coolidge lit the first national Christmas tree in 1923, establishing the annual Christmas tree-lighting ceremony by succeeding presidents. The "Nation's Christmas Tree" was dedicated in 1925 at King's Canyon National Park in California. This giant sequoia tree, named in honor of General Grant, is 40 feet thick and 275 feet tall. Yuletide services are held at its base at high noon every Christmas Day.

Optional applications for "Home for Christmas"

1. After telling the story, review the things that were folded from paper, using the names from the story: scarf, chiseling tool, snow-shoes, backpack, etc. *(auditory sequential memory)*. Construct the tree again using a fresh, unfolded square of paper *(visual sequential memory)*. Ask the group to tell you which fold comes next and recite the name of each step aloud to reinforce the folding sequence. Distribute squares of paper for individual folding *(kinesthetic sequential memory)*. Fold together, step-by-step, or assist only when needed.

2. Decorate the trees and predict where the markings will be when the model is un-folded. Unfold to check the predictions. Try decorating another unfolded square, then construct the tree. Did the markings fall into place where they should be or were they way off *(analysis, synthesis)*?

3. Use the origami trees as part of a three dimensional holiday display or as nametags, glue them to earrings or lace with yarn for holiday necklaces, insert small cups inside and fill with candies, insert a candle holder or vase inside for holiday flowers, or hang them as holiday ornaments. Try using holi-day wrapping paper for variety *(application)*.

4. Research and discuss the various legends relating to the origin of Christmas trees.

Which are documented and which are purely folklore? How have Christmas trees changed throughout the years? How do they differ in various countries? What other Christmas traditions originated with the Germans *(analysis, evaluation)*?

5. Write an original legend or folk tale that explains the origin of Christmas trees. Make it far-fetched or incorporate actual historical facts. Illustrate with original drawings, paperfolding or other crafts *(synthesis)*.

6. Present this story as a play. Choose a narrator and actors to play Martin, Uncle Hermann, and Aunt Elsa. Fold a giant tree from large wrapping paper or art paper (synthesis).

7. Construct trees of various sizes. Making increasingly smaller trees improves skill and precision. Solve this equation: If an 8.5" square yields a tree that's 5" wide, how wide is a tree made from a 4" square *(analysis)*?

8. Use this story to introduce or complement discussions or units about:
   a. German influence in America and throughout the world.
   b. Pioneer life styles.
   c. Homemade toys and gifts.
   d. Personal holiday memories or traditions.
   e. Neighbors and families helping each other.

Date	Group	Notes

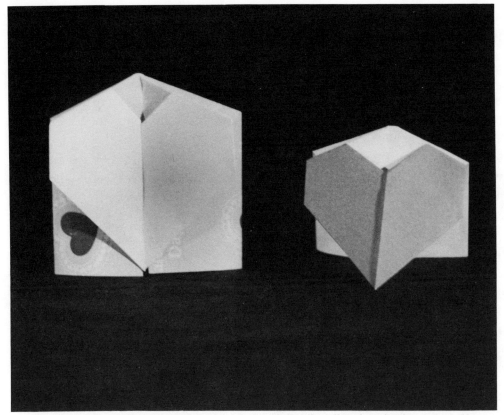

These versatile hearts are folded in just six steps. Folding directions begin on page 53.

THE SINGING ROOFER OF FRANCE

About the story:

A young singer is in love with a woman whose family owns a roofing business. She will not marry him unless he can repair a roof as well as she can. But who will allow a singer to work on his roof? A famous fashion designer gives him a chance!

Recommended ages: Listening only - age 3 through adult.
Listening and folding - age 5 through adult.

Required materials:

One square of paper at least six inches on each side, folded into a heart and then completely unfolded for storytelling.

Optional introductory statement:

I'm going to tell you a story about a man who makes clothes, who helps a man who sings songs, who loves a woman who fixes roofs. Watch carefully as I fold this square (hold up the unfolded origami heart) into various shapes. This is called origami, or Japanese paperfolding. The name of the story is "The Singing Roofer of France".

The Singing Roofer of France

In the famous fashion city of Paris, France, there lives an unusual designer named Pierre Pierre. He has the ability to look into your heart to see exactly what kind of person you really are and also, what you want most out of life. As he studies you, an idea for an outfit that's exactly right for you pops into his mind. As a special trademark, Pierre Pierre always sews a simple little heart into every piece of clothing that he creates. He likes to hide it, so that only his finest and most careful customers can find it.

One day, a strong and handsome young man was walking slowly down the streets of Paris, singing a little folk song softly to himself. His eyes never wavered from studying the roof tops of all the little shops. But he stopped singing when he saw the roof of Pierre Pierre's shop. For the longest time, the young man just stood there on the sidewalk, staring up at the roof. He seemed to be thinking very hard.

Finally, Pierre Pierre came out to ask him what was wrong.

"I couldn't help noticing that your roof is sagging," said the young man. "It is the first bad roof that I've seen today." *(Demonstrate with fold #1).*

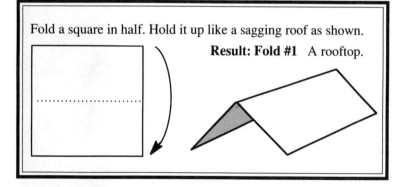

Fold a square in half. Hold it up like a sagging roof as shown.

Result: Fold #1   A rooftop.

"Oui," agreed Pierre Pierre. "It is terrible. The rain leaks through the cracks. I have to put pots and pans around my showroom to catch the water."

"I will be happy to fix it for you," said the young man.

"You will? How wonderful! What is your price?" asked the famous clothes maker.

"I need three things. I need food to strengthen my arms, so that I can pound a straight nail. I need good clean water to moisten my throat, so that I can sing a strong song. And I need a place to rest so that I can finish your roof as quickly as possible."

"That's all that you want? Only room and board? Why is your price so low?"

Looking down with embarrassment, the young man admitted, "I'm not a very experienced roofer. Actually, I'm a singer, not a roofer at all. In fact, I've never repaired a roof before in my life. But if I become a roofer, then my girlfriend has agreed to marry me. You see, everyone in her family is in the roofing business. And she won't marry anyone who can't fix a roof as well as she can. I think that if I learn roofing, I can be both a singer and a roofer. I can be a singing roofer."

Pierre Pierre looked into the young man's heart and saw immediately that he was honest and hopelessly in love. The roof over the famous designer's shop was in such terrible condition, that even if the young man completely botched the job, it couldn't possibly get any worse. So Pierre Pierre agreed to give the young man his start in the roofing business.

The young man went right to work, singing his heart out as he pounded nails into new boards and shingles. In only two days, he fixed the leaks and made the roof good and straight like this (*demonstrate with fold #2*):

"I am almost finished," he announced proudly. "Before I leave, I want to thank you for taking a chance on me. I found out that I love fixing roofs! I never realized how terrific my singing sounds from up on top of the city! But, with your permission, there is one change I would like to make. I think you need a section carved out of your roof where you can add a window and flower box. I will show you what I mean."

The young man broke into a loud and merry tune as he made shutters on each of the corners of the roof, like this (*demonstrate with fold #3*):

While the young roofer put his tools away, Pierre Pierre was finishing a new cape that he had designed as a special wedding surprise for the young man's bride. All he had to do was add the sides like this (*demonstrate with fold # 4*):

"She will love it!" sang the young man. "But how will I ever keep it looking new and beautiful until our wedding day? She has not even agreed to marry me, yet."

"Do not worry. Simply fold it in half like this," said Pierre Pierre. (*Demonstrate with fold #5*).

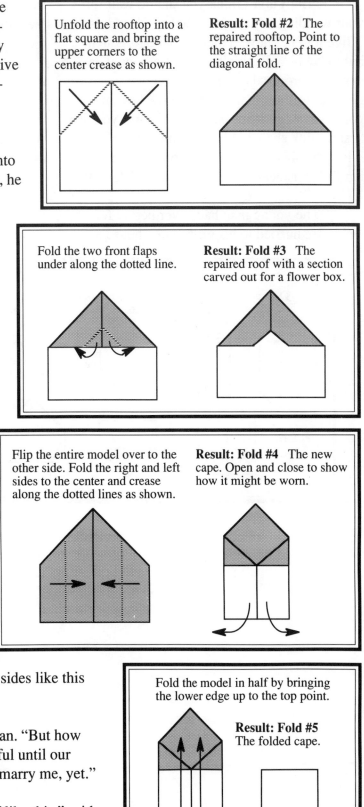

Unfold the rooftop into a flat square and bring the upper corners to the center crease as shown.

Result: Fold #2 The repaired rooftop. Point to the straight line of the diagonal fold.

Fold the two front flaps under along the dotted line.

Result: Fold #3 The repaired roof with a section carved out for a flower box.

Flip the entire model over to the other side. Fold the right and left sides to the center and crease along the dotted lines as shown.

Result: Fold #4 The new cape. Open and close to show how it might be worn.

Fold the model in half by bringing the lower edge up to the top point.

Result: Fold #5 The folded cape.

"But I don't think you should wait for your wedding day to give it to her," he advised. "Give it to her now. You may have forgotten, but today is Valentine's Day, a traditional day of marriage proposals. I promise you that when you give her this new cape, she will see how much you love her and will be eager to marry you. But first, I think she would be charmed if we folded it into the shape of a roof to represent her family's business." *(Demonstrate with fold #6).*

The young man had never before felt so lucky. He hurried to his girlfriend's house and rushed right in to present her with his Valentine's Day gift.

(Flip the model over to the back side so that the heart is facing up.)

She was thrilled and offered him a surprise of her own. "Will you marry me?" she asked.

Of course, the young man sang out, "Oui, oui!" And to this day, he is the happiest singing roofer in all of France.

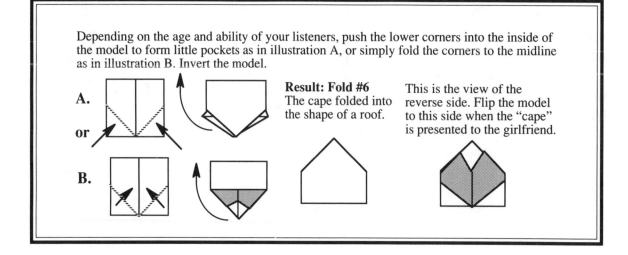

Depending on the age and ability of your listeners, push the lower corners into the inside of the model to form little pockets as in illustration A, or simply fold the corners to the midline as in illustration B. Invert the model.

A.

or

B.

Result: Fold #6
The cape folded into the shape of a roof.

This is the view of the reverse side. Flip the model to this side when the "cape" is presented to the girlfriend.

Summary of folding directions:

Fold a square in half. Hold it up like a sagging roof as shown.

Result: Fold #1   A rooftop.

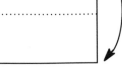
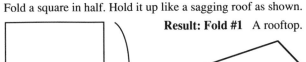

Unfold the rooftop into a flat square and bring the upper corners to the center crease as shown.

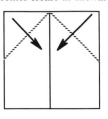

Result: Fold #2   The repaired rooftop. Point to the straight line of the diagonal fold.

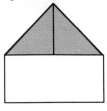

Fold the two front flaps under along the dotted line.

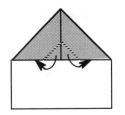

Result: Fold #3   The repaired roof with a section carved out for a flower box.

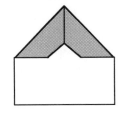

Flip the entire model over to the other side. Fold the right and left sides to the center and crease along the dotted lines as shown.

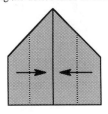

Result: Fold #4   The new cape. Open and close to show how it might be worn.

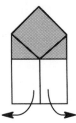

Fold the model in half by bringing the lower edge up to the top point.

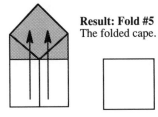

Result: Fold #5 The folded cape.

Depending on the age and ability of your listeners, push the lower corners into the inside of the model to form little pockets as in illustration A, or simply fold the corners to the midline as in illustration B. Invert the model.

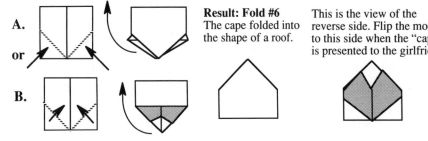

Result: Fold #6 The cape folded into the shape of a roof.

This is the view of the reverse side. Flip the model to this side when the "cape" is presented to the girlfriend.

Why do we exchange hearts?

Most scholars believe that Valentine's Day originated with the ancient Roman holiday, Lupercalia, a holiday dedicated to young lovers. Young men placed names of young women into a box and drew at random. The resulting couples were considered betrothed and remained together until the next Lupercalia, traditionally set on Feb. 15. In 496 A.D., Pope Galasius of Rome changed Lupercalia to St. Valentine's Day, to be celebrated on Feb. 14.

There are three "Valentines" who were prominent in church history, but it is unknown which one was the intended namesake for this holiday. A Christian priest named Valentine was stoned to death on Feb. 14 in the year 270 A. D. A legend about his imprisonment says that he left a farewell note for the jailer's little daughter who he had cured of blindness. He signed it "from your Valentine." Another legend says that this same priest defied the orders of Emperor Claudius by secretly performing marriage rites for young couples. The men did not want to leave their young wives and refused to become soldiers for Claudius' wars, so the monarch threw Valentine in prison, where he died. The beloved Bishop of Umbria, was also named Valentine and was martyred in the last part of the third century. A third Valentine died in Africa.

The old custom of drawing names on St. Valentine's Eve continued in England. When a young man drew a girl's name, he wore it on his sleeve, and courted and protected her during the following year. They exchanged love tokens. Only men gave presents, usually simple bouquets of flowers. Later, more elaborate, lacy

valentines and heart-shaped candies became popular. Balls were scheduled for St. Valentine's Eve.

As St. Valentine's Day became more popular, many customs and superstitions emerged. During Elizabethan times, it was thought that unmarried persons would find their true love in the first person of the opposite sex encountered and greeted with the words, "Good morning, 'tis Saint Valentine's Day." Young man carried bachelor buttons in their pockets on Valentine's Day. If the flower lived throughout the day, he would marry his current sweetheart. If it died, he would seek another. In some English towns, little children used to go about singing St. Valentine songs and collecting small gifts. Valentines were also placed on friends' doorsteps. There was an old saying that if snowdrops were brought into the house before Feb. 14, the single women of that house would remain unmarried all year. On St. Valentine's Eve, some girls pinned bay leaves to the four corners of their pillows and one in the middle. If they dreamed about their sweethearts, then they would be married that year.

In Derbyshire, the girls used to look through the keyhole early on the morning of St. Valentine's Day and if they saw only a single object or person, they would remain unmarried all that year. If they saw two or more objects or persons, they would be sure to have a sweetheart, and if they were lucky enough to see a rooster or a hen, then they would certainly be married before the year was out. There was also a belief that a girl would see her future husband if she ran around the church twelve times at midnight repeating, "I sow hempseed, hempseed I sow, He that loves me best come after me now."

The first commercial valentines appeared around 1800 and with advanced printing technology, mechanical reproductions were possible by 1840. In 1830, Miss Ester Howland, one of America's first female entrepreneurs, began importing lace, fine papers, and other supplies for her new valentine business. Sales of her "Worchester" valentines amounted to $100,000 per year. By the time of the Civil War, Valentine's Day ranked next to Christmas in holiday importance. Styles and tastes have shifted throughout the years, and many of the earlier valentines have become collectors' items.

Popular Valentine's Symbols:

Love birds: stems from a medieval folk tradition that maintained that the springtime mating of birds occurs on February 14.

Hearts: a symbol of love and emotion since early Roman times. It was considered the seat of love and affection in Western Europe as early as the 12th century.

Roses: historically the flower of romance and represented Eros, the Roman god of love.

Lace: comes from a Latin word meaning to "snare" or "noose".

Cupid: Roman mythological god whose name in Latin means "desire". He possessed a bow with a quiver of arrows by which he transfixed the hearts of young men and maidens.

Cherubs: descendents of Cupid, without bow and arrows.

Optional applications for "The Singing Roofer of France"

1. After telling the story, review the steps necessary to repair the roof and complete the cape, using the names from the story for each step *(auditory sequential memory)*. Construct the origami valentine again using a fresh, unfolded square of paper. Point out how to line up the edges and press down firmly *(visual sequential memory)*. To reinforce their memory, ask the group to tell you which step comes next. Repeat the names of the folds aloud in unison. When the group is confident of the folding sequence, distribute squares of paper for individual folding *(kinesthetic memory)*. Fold together, step-by-step, or assist only when needed.

2. Write poems or messages inside the flaps of the heart. Exchange the hearts as Valentine's Day cards, or use as nametags, placemarks, or as part of a Valentine's Day display *(synthesis)*.

3. Research the history of Valentine's Day cards. Decorate the origami valentines with different colors and materials, following styles prevalent in specific historical periods. Pay special attention to the homemade cards exchanged before 1850. Label each card according to its era, displaying them chronologically *(analysis, synthesis)*.

4. Make hearts of various sizes and textures. Hold a contest to see who can fold the smallest hearts, the fastest, the most symmetrical, the largest, the heaviest, the most colorful, the most authentic, etc. Make a category so that everyone is a winner *(application, synthesis)*.

5. Make predictions about what size hearts can be built from what size squares. Form the equation: if an 8.5" square yields a 4.25" heart, what size heart will a 6" square make? Test the accuracy of your ratios *(analysis)*.

6. Play Valentine party games:

    a. **Friend, Friend, Heart**: play the same way as "Duck, Duck, Goose", only have each child say "Friend" as they circle and tap the heads of the others. When they tap the head of the child they want to be chased by, they give them the heart, run around the circle and sit down in the spot vacated by that child, who then circles and taps, giving the heart to the next person.

    b. **Pin the Heart**: Blindfold a child, spin him, and see if he can pin (or tape) his heart onto the heart of the figure of a person stapled to a bulletin board.

    c. **Pass the Heart**: Exchange valentines by passing them to the rhythm of a song. When the music stops, the valentine you are holding is the one that you keep. You become that person's special friend for the day, being extra considerate to him or performing little favors.

    d. **Heart Toss**: Make a large target heart and place it in the center of a circle of children. Each child takes a turn flipping their origami hearts (Frisbee style) at the target. The one who comes closest gets to be the next leader or is the first one to be served Valentine treats.

    e. **Hide the Heart**: All children put their heads down while one child hides his heart. The children take turns guessing where it is. The one who guesses the location of the heart, is the next one to hide their heart.

Date	Group	Notes

This friendly bunny can be used as a puppet or a hat. Folding directions begin on page 61.

About the story:

Queen Hen consults Sly Fox about what to do with the unusually large number of colored eggs being produced on Rainbow Mountain. Sly Fox suggests that they be shared with all the people of the world, so King Beard sponsors a race. The winner is given the job of delivering the eggs.

Recommended ages: Listening only - age 3 through adult.
Listening and folding - age 5 through adult.

Required materials:

A marking pen, and one square of paper at least six inches on each side, folded into a bunny and then completely unfolded for storytelling. <u>Note</u>: do not draw the bunny's facial features before the story is told. Wait until that point in the story to add the face.

Optional introductory statement:

I'm going to tell you a story about a magical place called Rainbow Mountain. Watch carefully as I fold this square (hold up the unfolded origami bunny) into various shapes. This is called origami, or Japanese paperfolding. The name of the story is "The Rabbits of Rainbow Mountain".

The Rabbits of Rainbow Mountain

One spring, a long, long time ago, everything seemed to be fine and beautiful on Rainbow Mountain. The mountain laurel and honeysuckle burst into bloom just when they were supposed to. The grass greened after a hard rain and the wind whispered sweet secrets to all the newborn leaves and flowers. But everything was not as fine as it seemed, for Queen Hen, the most important bird on the mountain, discovered a serious problem. *(Hold up fold #1).*

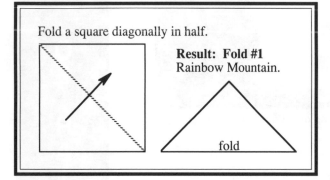

Fold a square diagonally in half.

Result: Fold #1
Rainbow Mountain.

fold

Here, *(point to various places on the mountain slope)* hidden in the forests and caves of Rainbow Mountain were hundreds of brightly colored hens who laid thousands of brightly colored eggs.

"Blue hens! Yellow hens! Green, orange, red, and purple hens! All hens of Rainbow Mountain!" declared Queen Hen. "We have a terrible problem! There are too many eggs this year!"

"Too many eggs! Too many eggs!" clucked the hens.

"We must gather our best eggs and take them to Sly Fox. She always has good ideas. She will know what to do with them."

So the hens gathered their most colorful eggs and placed them gently in a big box that looked like this *(demonstrate with fold #2):*

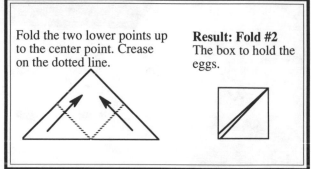

Fold the two lower points up to the center point. Crease on the dotted line.

Result: Fold #2
The box to hold the eggs.

Queen Hen and several of the strongest hens carried the precious box to Sly Fox, who lived further up on Rainbow Mountain. *(Demonstrate with fold #3):*

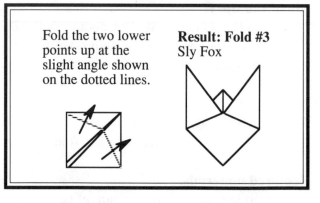

Fold the two lower points up at the slight angle shown on the dotted lines.

Result: Fold #3
Sly Fox

"What beautiful eggs!" gasped sly fox. "And look at how the shells sparkle in the sunshine. These eggs are much too pretty to eat for breakfast. What are you going to do with them, Queen Hen?"

"I was hoping that you would have an idea," she clucked.

"We could give them to wise King Beard who lives at the top of the mountain. He sees everything in the world from up there. He would know what to do with such wonderful eggs."

So Queen Hen and her helpers, and Sly Fox and her helpers, all carried the big box of colored eggs to the top of the mountain and presented them to wise King Beard. *(Demonstrate with fold #4)*:

On the word "top", fold only the upper layer to the top point and crease along the dotted line. Point to the top point as though it represents the mountain top where King Beard lives. Then fold part of the ears to the back of the model along the dotted lines as shown.

Result: Fold #4 King Beard.

"Ah!" sighed King Beard when he opened the box. "These eggs are as glorious as any of our mountain flowers. If we tossed them into the sky, the people of the world would be surprised to see a rainbow that appeared without any rain! It would be fun to fool them! It would take them a couple years to unravel this mystery!"

"But King Beard," clucked Queen Hen, "The eggs would surely break if we threw them up into the air, and so would the hearts of all our colored hens who laid them. Isn't there another way we could celebrate without smashing the eggs?"

"I have an idea," said Sly Fox. "Let's pass them out to all the people in the world. We always feel happy about spring coming, so we can share our happiness by sharing our eggs. When the people see all these bright colors, they will know why we're called Rainbow Mountain."

"An excellent suggestion," agreed King Beard. "On the eve of the first Sunday after the full moon in March, we will have a great race. The fastest animals on Rainbow Mountain will be chosen to pass out the colored eggs to all the people in the world."

Soon the day of the great mountain race arrived. The animals had to run all the way around the mountain, through long grasses, thorny brambles, gooey mud puddles, and thick bushes.

King Beard shouted, "Get ready! Get set! Go!"

He had never seen such a sight! All different kinds of animals crawled, slithered, hopped, ran, and leaped away as fast as they could.

The deer dashed way out in front of the others and were winning the race until they stopped to graze in the grasses. The deer ate so much that they were too full to race any more. Then the cougars took over the lead until they snagged their silky ears in the thorny brambles and sat down to pout. The raccoons led for a while until they paused to look for shells in the mud puddles. The foxes were ahead until they scratched their noses in the thick bushes. Finally, one group of animals sprang into the lead and were well ahead for the rest of the race! *(Hold up fold #5)*.

When these cheerful little rabbits burst through the finish line, the hens crowed their approval and gave each of them a big basket of colorful eggs. Late that night, the rabbits of Rainbow Mountain hopped down from the hills to deliver the eggs to all the houses. They worked quickly and carefully, so when the first bright rays of Easter sunshine burst out from behind the hills, every doorstep glittered and glowed like a rainbow, all lit up with the brilliant colors of the beautiful eggs.

The people liked their colorful eggs so much that the rabbits delivered them every spring at the same time, early in the morning on the first Sunday after the full moon in March,

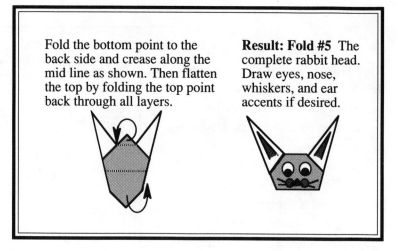

Fold the bottom point to the back side and crease along the mid line as shown. Then flatten the top by folding the top point back through all layers.

Result: Fold #5 The complete rabbit head. Draw eyes, nose, whiskers, and ear accents if desired.

Easter Sunday. The rabbits of Rainbow Mountain eventually became known as Easter rabbits, and King Beard, Queen Hen, Sly Fox, and all the colorful hens of Rainbow Mountain were very proud of them indeed. After all, it isn't every day that glittering rainbows appear on doorsteps without even the first drop of rain.

Summary of folding directions:

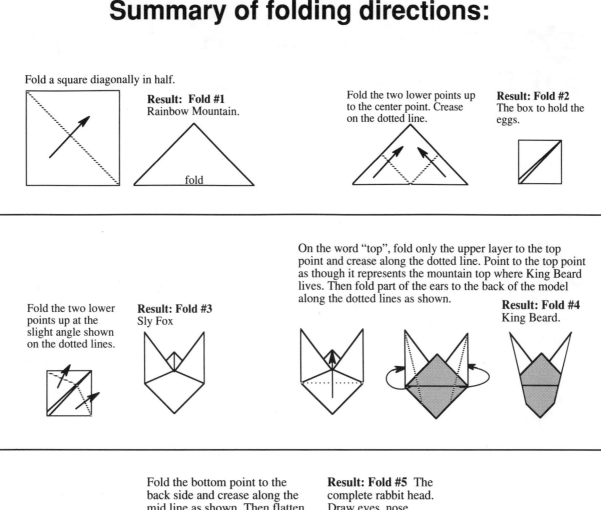

Fold a square diagonally in half.

Result: Fold #1
Rainbow Mountain.

fold

Fold the two lower points up
to the center point. Crease
on the dotted line.

Result: Fold #2
The box to hold the
eggs.

Fold the two lower
points up at the
slight angle shown
on the dotted lines.

Result: Fold #3
Sly Fox

On the word "top", fold only the upper layer to the top
point and crease along the dotted line. Point to the top point
as though it represents the mountain top where King Beard
lives. Then fold part of the ears to the back of the model
along the dotted lines as shown.

Result: Fold #4
King Beard.

Fold the bottom point to the
back side and crease along the
mid line as shown. Then flatten
the top by folding the top point
back through all layers.

Result: Fold #5 The
complete rabbit head.
Draw eyes, nose,
whiskers, and ear
accents if desired.

HOLIDAY HISTORY

Why do rabbits bring eggs?

Easter → moon → hares → eggs → Easter rabbit

Easter is a lunar holiday because it is celebrated on the first Sunday after the full moon in March. Rather than designate a specific date, the timing of Easter celebrations varies each year according to the moon.

Throughout history, many associations have been made between the moon and hares, a relative of rabbits. Japanese artists painted the hare across the moon's disc and the Chinese represented the moon as a hare pounding rice in a mortar. Ancient Europeans believed that both the moon and the hare represented fertility. Three characteristics of the hare probably led to this associations:

1. The hare is born with eyes wide open, suggestive of the full moon.
2. Hares are very prolific animals. The female carries her young for one month, the length of a complete moon cycle.
3. Hares are nocturnal. Like the moon, they come out at night.

The customs surrounding the modern Easter rabbit originated in old Germany where the "Easter Hare" behaved like a springtime St. Nicholas, bringing gifts to good little German children. There are two possible explanations for why rabbits replaced hares in North Ameri-

can Easter celebrations. It was either a linguistic accident which occurred during translation or was due to the fact that hares are not native to North America, but rabbits are.

Easter rabbits bring eggs because the egg was one of the symbols associated with the Anglo-Saxon fertility goddess, Eostre. Ancient pre-Christian people worshipped nature and celebrated Eostre in the springtime. They ate sacramental cakes made from eggs in honor of their fertility goddess. Many pre-Christian cultures also believed that the universe was derived from the egg, a symbol of rebirth and regeneration. This concept fit well with the Christian theme of resurrection, so the symbol was retained in Easter celebrations. With both the hare and egg used symbolically in the spring, it was natural for the two symbols to be combined in Easter rabbit traditions.

The practice of dyeing and decorating eggs was probably introduced to Europeans by crusaders returning from the Middle East. Ancient Egyptians, Persians, Phoenicians, Greeks and Romans commonly dyed and exchanged eggs during their springtime festivals. Egg rolling, egg hunting and decorating egg trees are now common Easter practices throughout the Western world.

Optional applications for
"The Rabbits of Rainbow Mountain"

1. After telling the story, review the things that were folded from paper, using the names from the story: the mountain, the egg box, Sly Fox, etc. *(auditory sequential memory)*. Construct the rabbit again using a fresh, unfolded square of paper *(visual sequential memory)*. Ask the group to tell you which step comes next to reinforce their memory. Have them say the names of each step aloud in unison. When they are confident of the folding sequence, distribute squares of paper for individual folding *(kinesthetic memory)*. Fold together, step-by-step, or assist only when needed.

2. Decorate the rabbit heads and predict where the markings will be when the model is unfolded. Unfold to check the predictions. Try decorating another unfolded square, then construct the rabbit. Did the markings fall into place where they should be or were they way off *(analysis, synthesis)*?

3. Construct finger puppets by starting with two or three inch squares of paper. Make several for each person. Folding with smaller paper encourages greater precision and results in increased pride and confidence. Use the finger puppets in Easter plays, parades, relays, or in the following finger play:

Five little bunnies marching in a line,
One got tired and started to whine.
Four little bunnies dancing up and down,
One tipped over and made a frown.
Three little bunnies swaying to and fro,
One got hungry and said, "I have to go!"
Two little bunnies holding hands,
One let go, saying, "I have other plans."
One little bunny standing all alone,
He felt sad and just went home.
Come back, bunnies! Come and play!
Let's pretend it's a brand new day.

(put the finger puppets back on and repeat)

4. Make bunny hats from newspaper or wrapping paper, starting with 20 or 22 inch squares. Act out the finger play in suggestion #3, pantomiming the facial expressions and motions. Repeat with a new group of bunnies until everyone has a turn. Video tape and play back during snack time.

5. Try folding the ears into different shapes and positions in folding step #3. What other animals are suggested by the new ear lengths and shapes? Add appropriate facial features. Make a mobile of all the different animals *(synthesis)*.

6. Ask the group to invent new stories or plays about how Easter rabbit traditions may have started. Work individually or in small groups. Present at an Easter party *(synthesis)*.

7. Discuss the problem solving techniques used by the characters in the story. Were the solutions successful? How else could the excess eggs have been disposed of? What feelings or emotions had to be considered? Did the characters work well together? What roles did they have? Was a race the best way to choose who would deliver the eggs? How did the losers feel? What else could King Beard have done? If you were Queen Hen, Sly Fox, or King Beard, what would you have done differently? Give reasons *(analysis, evaluation)*.

8. Dance the "Bunny Hop" wearing bunny hats or bunny finger puppets.

Date	Group	Notes

This attractive basket can be arranged in two positions. Folding directions begin on page 71.

About the story:

Despite tough odds, Anne Fowler decides to reform herself and works to overcome a reputation for bad behavior. Her dream comes true when she is chosen to reign over the village May Day festivities.

Recommended ages: Listening only - age 5 through adult.

Listening and folding - age 7 through adult.

Required materials:

One square of paper at least six inches on each side, folded into a basket and then completely unfolded for storytelling.

Optional introductory statement:

I'm going to tell you an amazing story that happened 300 years ago in a tiny village in England. Watch carefully as I fold this square (hold up the unfolded origami basket) into various shapes. This is called origami, or Japanese paperfolding. Before we get started, do you have any questions? (pause) The name of the story is "Queen of May".

Queen of May

About 300 years ago, in the village of Kendal in the Lake District of England, there lived a girl named Anne Fowler. She had the bad luck to be the only girl in a family of seven children. Her three older brothers were the roughest bullies in the village and her three younger brothers were the terrors of their humble farm. Unfortunately, Anne's father was often the most stubborn and short tempered of them all. Her mother, her only friend and confidant, died of fever when Anne was only ten. At thirteen, Anne was becoming a young woman, and she missed her mother more than ever.

The Fowler boys were so nasty and mean that the people of Kendal had renamed them the Scowler boys. Anne's brothers bullied everyone into obeying even their most ridiculous demands. The villagers were disgusted with them, but usually gave in to make them go away. The other boys sang songs like this:

"Scowler Fowlers came to town,
 knocked the lassies to the ground.
All the good folk chased them down
 and beat them all sound and round."

Poor Anne was called the "She Scowler" and no one would be her friend or even talk to her. With this kind of treatment, she began to act like a scowler. Her voice was too loud. Her words were rude. Her mouth was always frowning. And she never just walked anywhere. Instead, she slammed things down and stomped clumsily about, her shoulders knotted up with anger and self-pity. She didn't bother to comb and braid her hair like the other girls in Kendal and with all the work that was required of her at home, she scarcely had time to scrub the soot from her face, let alone see to it that her clothes were clean and mended.

The only times that Anne knew any happiness were the rare evenings when the family had worked so hard that they were too tired to fight before turning in for the night.

"Tell me the story about when Mum was the queen of May," she would say to her father.

Her father's eyes would get misty as he gazed far into the past, back to his brash and faultless youth, back to when he was the strongest and wittiest lad in Kendal.

"Ah, lass, your Mum was as pretty as posies and as pure as rain. She was made from the best of everything. Her hair was gold, piles of gold heaped up so high that the lord of the Manor wanted to tax it. Her eyes were sapphires, rich and deep, and her lips....ah, lass, her lips were rose petals moist with morning dew." He always paused and sighed here before he told the rest of the story.

"And in her 13th year, the lord of the Manor glimpsed her as she slipped through the wood, gathering flowers and singing her morning songs. He asked her name and ne'er forgot it. For when May Day came and we all got up early to go a-greening and a-gathering and to cut the tallest Maypole of all time, the lord, he called out your Mum's name to be queen of May. So there she sat, up on the throne, the flowers round her head. We all danced round the Maypole 'til night and it t'was your old Dad she picked out that day. Fowler fleet, Fowler quick, the fastest stepping dancing feet..."

But then as he remembered this, the best day of his life, his eyes would harden and the twisted scowl that imprisoned his face would return. Sensing a chance to take control, the boys would chant:

> "Anne, Anne the ugly bug.
> Pig queen, goat queen, bad and mean.
> Anne, Anne the ugly bug
> Ugh! Ugh! Ugh!"

Anne would fly at them with fists and nails, her rage choking out the sobs that would come later after her father stopped the fighting by blowing out the light and ordering them all to bed.

After one of these evenings in early March, Anne covered herself like this *(demonstrate the covering actions with a full square of paper used like a blanket)* and crammed her fist into her mouth to muffle the hopeless weeping that only sleep would silence. That night she had a strange, but vivid dream. She saw herself skipping lightly through the woods, gathering spring flowers into a satchel that looked like this *(demonstrate with fold #1)*:

She sang in a sweet voice very different from her own, and as she danced, long strands of silky yellow hair swirled around her. Finally she came to rest beneath a tall fir tree that looked like this *(demonstrate with fold #2)*:

As she leaned back against the tree, she began to sing this song:

> "Queen of May, I will be
> if I help all that I see.
> 60 days until May Day,
> 60 deeds that I must pay.
> 60 days of kindness will
> put me on that royal hill.
> Queen of May, for a day,
> only 60 days away!"

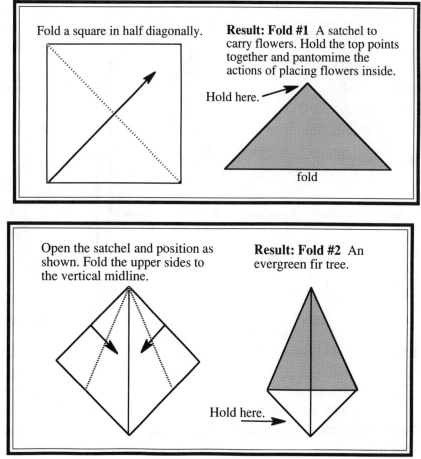

Fold a square in half diagonally.

Result: Fold #1 A satchel to carry flowers. Hold the top points together and pantomime the actions of placing flowers inside.

Hold here.

fold

Open the satchel and position as shown. Fold the upper sides to the vertical midline.

Result: Fold #2 An evergreen fir tree.

Hold here.

When Anne awoke, she was chanting, "60 days, 60 deeds, 60 days, 60 deeds..."

In the dark gloom of their shabby little farm hut, she whispered her promise, "I will do it, Mum! I will be Queen of May!"

The first day after her dream was as difficult as any she had ever faced. Nothing went right. The bread wouldn't rise. The butter wouldn't curdle. Her youngest brother, Little Will, dropped a basketful of eggs and when he kicked over her wash bucket, she had had enough. Anne screeched and took off after him. Just as she was about to squeeze her hands around his skinny little neck, she glanced down to see this lone sprig of green grass poking up through the rocks *(demonstrate with fold #3)*:

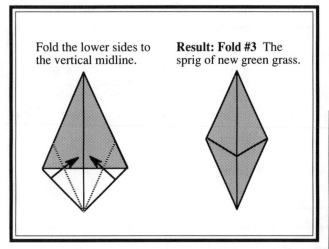

Fold the lower sides to the vertical midline.

Result: Fold #3 The sprig of new green grass.

Spring is coming, it seemed to say.

60 days, 60 deeds, she thought to herself.

Anne took a deep breath and released Little Will. "Do you want me to play tag with you?" she offered.

He looked at her with deep suspicion. "You'll kick me," he muttered, still panting from the chase.

"No...I'll show you how to play the same way that Mum showed me," she said. He agreed and her first good deed was done.

The next day, her second youngest brother, Small Jack, left the hen house door open and she had to chase and gather all the hens, a tiresome chore that she didn't want to do. She was planning to ambush him when he came in for a drink of water, but then she remembered her promise.

"59 days, 59 deeds," she whispered.

So instead of jumping on Small Jack and pulling his hair out, Anne offered to build him a seesaw on the big rock next to the well. "I'll make it the way Mum made one for me," she said.

She dragged a log out of the woods and balanced it on the rock so that it bobbed up and down like this *(demonstrate with fold #4)*:

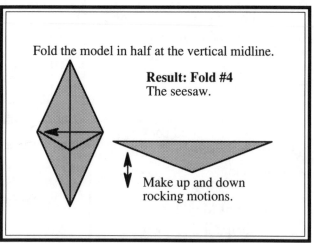

Fold the model in half at the vertical midline.

Result: Fold #4 The seesaw.

Make up and down rocking motions.

Small Jack giggled so loudly when Anne pushed him up and down, that Little Will ran over to join the fun. When they tired of the seesaw, Will taught Jack to play tag. Another day, another deed.

The next day, Anne woke up early. It was unusually warm and sunny, so Anne decided to take a walk through the woods before her brothers got up and began demanding something to eat. Not far from home, she heard a desperate cry for help. It was a baby woodpecker *(demonstrate with fold #5)*, fallen from its nest. She lifted it gently in the palm of her hand and brought it to her lips.

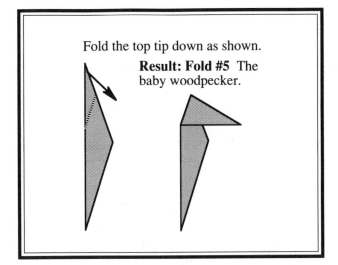

Fold the top tip down as shown.
Result: Fold #5 The baby woodpecker.

"Don't be afraid, little one," she whispered. The bird's frightened eyes met hers. It seemed to understand and stopped screeching. She put the baby woodpecker back in its nest and went back home. Another day, another deed.

The day after, Anne offered to help a little neighbor girl brush out her long ponytails that looked like this *(demonstrate with fold #6)*. She braided them neatly and tied them back with little red ribbons.

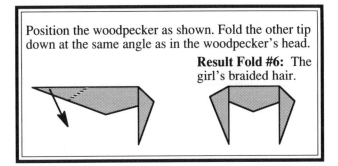

Position the woodpecker as shown. Fold the other tip down at the same angle as in the woodpecker's head.
Result Fold #6: The girl's braided hair.

After only a week of doing a good deed every day, Anne began to notice good things happening in her life. Now that her younger brothers knew some games to play, they didn't get into so much mischief and she was able to get all the cooking and cleaning done in record time. That left her with more time to mend her clothes and keep her hair washed and combed. After a month of kindness, she held her head high when she walked to the village with her shining golden hair and neatly stitched skirts. Amazingly, people greeted her and called out her name. And when they spoke kindly to her, it was easy to return their good will. She thought of several little favors to do for them, and never asked for thanks or payment of any kind.

Despite these changes in Anne's life, it was still the tradition in Kendal for the lord of the Manor to choose the May Day Queen. As the last days of April rushed by, she worried that she would be overlooked. She was only a simple farm girl and had never even spoken to anyone associated with the Manor House. How could she be selected if the lord did not even know her name?

On the last evening in April, the lord of the Manor stepped outside to look at the sunset before finishing preparations for the May Day feast. He had not yet made a decision about this year's Queen of May, so he planned to simply choose the first pretty lass that he saw the next morning. When he tried to return to the Manor House, a young woodpecker, still fluffy with downy feathers, landed on his sleeve.

"Anne Fowler," it chirped. "Choose Anne Fowler."

Startled, he jerked his arm away and the young bird flew back to the woods where Anne had saved it from its fall several weeks ago. The lord of the Manor believed in the magic of May, so the next day when the sun was at its highest peak and all the villagers were gathered around the Maypole to hear his proclamation, he followed the bird's advice.

"Pay homage, good folk, to our Queen of May! Pay homage to our fair Anne Fowler!"

The older Fowler boys, still as mean as ever, hooted and hollered at what they thought was a great May Day prank. But when they saw their sister, glowing and proud, come forward to accept this basket *(demonstrate with fold #7)*, they pushed through the crowd to be the first to honor her by kneeling and placing their delicate stems of wild roses into her regal basket.

"Pretty as posies, pure as rain," whispered Anne's father from beneath the towering Maypole. He sighed, his eyes misty, for at that very moment, he was experiencing the second best day of his life.

Unfold the girl's braids and position the model as shown. Lift each point up so that it turns inside out as it rises, collapsing inward on the existing creases. Pockets will form in each handle. Pull the tips of the handles together. Close them by twisting or folding the tips together. Tape if necessary.

Result: Fold #7 The complete May Day basket.

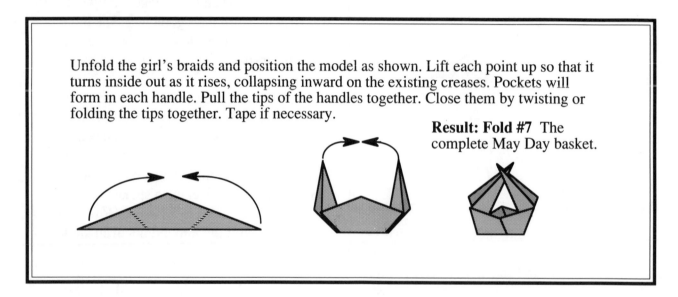

Summary of folding directions:

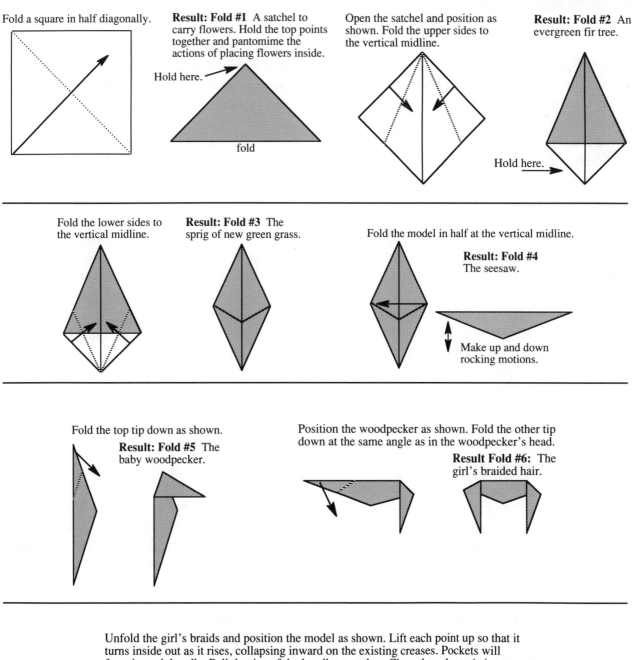

Fold a square in half diagonally.

Result: Fold #1 A satchel to carry flowers. Hold the top points together and pantomime the actions of placing flowers inside.

Hold here.

fold

Open the satchel and position as shown. Fold the upper sides to the vertical midline.

Result: Fold #2 An evergreen fir tree.

Hold here.

Fold the lower sides to the vertical midline.

Result: Fold #3 The sprig of new green grass.

Fold the model in half at the vertical midline.

Result: Fold #4 The seesaw.

Make up and down rocking motions.

Fold the top tip down as shown.

Result: Fold #5 The baby woodpecker.

Position the woodpecker as shown. Fold the other tip down at the same angle as in the woodpecker's head.

Result Fold #6: The girl's braided hair.

Unfold the girl's braids and position the model as shown. Lift each point up so that it turns inside out as it rises, collapsing inward on the existing creases. Pockets will form in each handle. Pull the tips of the handles together. Close them by twisting or folding the tips together. Tape if necessary.

Result: Fold #7 The complete May Day basket.

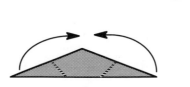

HOLIDAY HISTORY

Why go a-Maying?

Spring festivals were common in most ancient civilizations. Modern May Day traditions have their roots in the ancient Roman and Druid cultures, although the ancient Greeks were also influential with their annual festivals in honor of Chloris, the Greek goddess of flowers, and the spring athletic games where each victor received a crown of laurel leaves.

The Roman spring festival, Floralia, was dedicated to Flora, the Roman goddess of flowers. Instituted in Rome in 238 B. C., the Romans staged floral games and used blossoms in processions and dances from April 28 to May 3. Roman slaves were allowed to say and do as they pleased on May Day, as long as they returned to their master's house by evening.

The Druid festival, Beltane (Bel's fire) was held in honor of the Druid god, Bel. They lit fires in honor of the sun and to celebrate the return of light after the long winter. The Druids were also respectful of trees, particularly oak trees, which played important roles in Druid rites. When Rome occupied England, the two festivals merged, leading to modern May Day celebrations.

Traditionally, everyone in the village, regardless of their age, economic, or political stature, would go "a-maying" first thing in the morning. They would "bring home the May" by collecting boughs of greenery and fresh flowers, and then cut down the tallest Maypole that they could find. They'd wind through town in a colorful procession until they reached the village green where the Maypole was erected and decorated with streamers and fresh flowers. At noon, the lord of the manor announced the name of the young woman he had selected as the May queen. She sat in a throne of flowers and presided over the day's dancing, games, and contests. Other traditional activities included dancing around flower bedecked wells, driving decorated cows through the streets, washing young women's faces in May Day dew, and donning jester or Robin Hood costumes. These events varied according to individual village traditions.

The Maypoles usually stood for just one day, but some cities erected permanent ones. London had several that were adorned with flags, ribbons, and golden or brightly painted balls. The tallest, a 134 foot pole, was erected in 1661. It was bought by Sir Isaac Newton in 1717 to support a 124 foot telescope, the world's largest at that time. An old Hungarian legend tells about the first Maypole, or May Tree, as it was called in Hungary. May 1st is a Saint Day, dedicated to St. Philip and St. James. The story goes that on a May Day many centuries ago, a woman was walking with her staff when she was attacked by enemies and falsely accused of wrongdoing. She called upon the good Saints Philip and James to send some sign to prove her innocence. As soon as her prayer was uttered, her staff sprouted leaves and twigs. From then on, the May Tree was the symbolic center of May Day celebrations.

May Day festivities were forbidden in

England by the Parliament of 1644. The customs offended the Puritans, but this prohibition was repealed in 1661, leading to joyous May Day revivals. One of the first Maypoles in America was set up by Thomas Morton at his Merry Mount Plantation near Plymouth Colony in 1660. His men danced with the Indian squaws. This display of "cakes, ale, and the gay life" infuriated the Puritan Governor Endicott so much that he had the pole chopped down and stopped the festivities. He accused Morton of trading arms with the Indians and shipped him back to England.

May Day is still observed by hanging May baskets. This custom arose from the ancient belief that the baskets would keep evil spirits away. Fastening a bit of green to porches or doorways was also a way to bring a blessing to the house. Early practices saw children sneaking out in the darkness of May Day Eve to hang baskets filled with flowers and treats on doorknobs without being detected. But in more recent times, May baskets are presented openly as a tribute of love and friendliness.

May Day is celebrated as Lei Day in Hawaii. Flower garlands, or leis, are worn during special music, dancing, and pageantry. May Day is also known as a political holiday, a day devoted to the interests of labor groups and working men. Parades, labor demonstrations, and sporting events are staged.

Optional applications for "Queen of May"

1. After telling the story, review the steps necessary to fold the origami basket, using the names from the story: the satchel, the evergreen, the sprig of grass, etc. *(auditory sequential memory)*. Build the basket again using a fresh, unfolded square of paper *(visual sequential memory)*. Ask the group to tell you which step comes next. Recite the names of the steps aloud in unison. When the group is confident about the folding sequence, distribute squares of paper for individual folding *(kinesthetic memory)*. Fold together, step-by-step or assist only when needed.

2. Gather flowers or treats to place in the baskets and present to friends, family, neighbors, or shut-ins. Exchange baskets secretly within your group. Let the basket's contents represent something about the giver. Guess who the givers are and write thank you notes in return *(synthesis, analysis)*.

3. Make a giant basket from stiff wrapping paper or a grocery bag. Use it as a centerpiece for a May Day party or display. Decorate with ribbons and flowers. Determine the equation: if an 8.5" square makes a 4" basket, what size square will yield a 10"

basket *(analysis, synthesis)?*

4. Dramatize the story as part of a May Day pageant. Let a storyteller or narrator read the story as others act out the behaviors and say the words of Anne, the brothers, the baby woodpecker, the father and the townspeople. Let others take the part of the origami folder, using a large square that was been pre-folded for storytelling the usual way *(synthesis)*.

5. Discuss how our behaviors affect the behaviors of others, and how their actions affect our reactions. How do emotions influence behavior? How do expectations affect behavior? Is behavioral change possible? What is more effective, a change in actions or a change in words? Do actions really speak louder than words? Which characters do you feel sympathetic toward? Anne? Her father? Her older brothers? Her younger brothers? The townspeople? Examine the reasons for your answers *(evaluation, analysis)*.

6. Choose a character and write a story about him/her when he/she is five years older. How has he changed? How does he feel about his life? How does he relate to his family and neighborhood *(analysis, evaluation, synthesis)?*

7. Gather medieval folk music; construct and decorate a Maypole with flowers and streamers (use a coat rack indoors); and dance a simple ribbon dance where the partners weave their streamers in and out, over and under. Research and simulate other May Day customs *(analysis, synthesis, application)*

8. Hold May Day relays where team members take turns carrying small objects such as flowers, cotton balls, buttons, or pennies in the origami baskets. Baskets can be balanced or held in a variety of different silly ways *(application)*.

Date	Group	Notes

Words of sentiment turn this traditional lotus blossom into a special gift. Folding directions begin on page 79.

About the story:

Examining the most admired characteristics of motherhood leads to the invention of a surprise Mother's Day gift.

Recommended ages: Listening only - age 5 through adult.

Listening and folding - age 7 through adult.

Required materials:

A marking pen, and one square of paper at least eight inches on each side, folded through step #4. Large computer paper (eleven inches per side) works nicely. <u>Note</u>: Do not write the words or peel back the petals before storytelling.

Optional introductory statement:

Watch carefully as I fold this square (hold up the unfolded origami lotus blossom) into various shapes. This technique is called origami, or Japanese paperfolding. Before we get started, do you have any questions? (pause to answer questions, then launch right into the story text).

Mother's Day Surprise

Preliminary folds: Fold a square in half along the vertical midline, then fold the resulting rectangle in half along the horizontal midline. Completely unfold for storytelling.

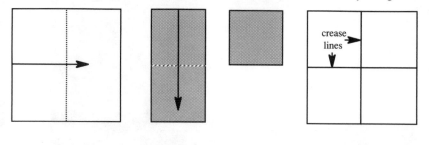

I was thinking that this year I'd like to give my mother a card that really represents my feelings for her. She is always saying how much she loves the things I make for her, so this year I'd like to make her something that expresses those special feelings.

What are the things that I do that show her that I love her? Perhaps I should write them down and send them to her. Let's see...I show my mother love by cooperating, by hugging and kissing, and by respecting her. *(Write "Hugs", "Kisses", "Cooperation", and "Respect" in each of the four corners as shown.)* If I fold all the corners in like this *(demonstrate with fold #1)*, then I can make an envelope for her card. *(Count 1 - 2 - 3 - 4 as you fold each corner in.)*

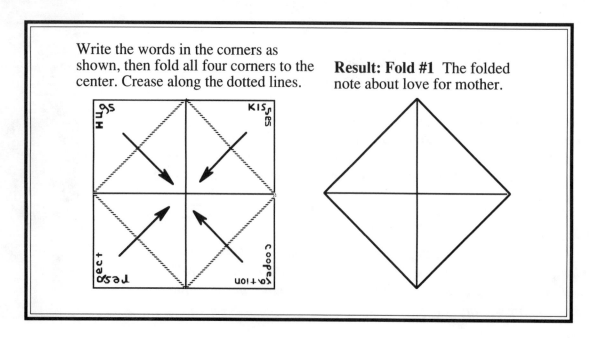

Write the words in the corners as shown, then fold all four corners to the center. Crease along the dotted lines.

Result: Fold #1 The folded note about love for mother.

But I also want my mother to know how fun she is and how I love to see her laugh and smile; and giggle and tickle. *(Write "Laughs", "Smiles", "Giggles", and "Tickles" in the four corners as shown.)* I'll fold it the same way I did before, making my own envelope. *(Count 1 - 2 - 3 - 4 as you fold each corner in.)*

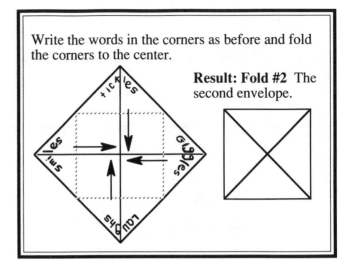

Write the words in the corners as before and fold the corners to the center.

Result: Fold #2 The second envelope.

My mother helps me in so many different ways, like when she listens to my problems, protects me from danger, comforts me when I'm sad, and cheers me on when I'm tackling something new. *(Write the words "listens", "protects", "comforts", and "cheers" in the corners as before for fold #3.)* I'll fold it up nice and tight just like I did before.

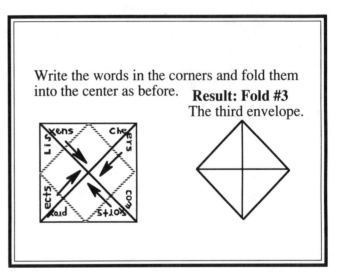

Write the words in the corners and fold them into the center as before. **Result: Fold #3** The third envelope.

I would like to surprise my mother but it is impossible to hide anything from her. Perhaps if I flipped this small envelope over and folded the corners to the center one last time, it would be small enough that she wouldn't notice it until I presented it on Mother's Day. *(Flip and fold the corners in as before for fold #4).*

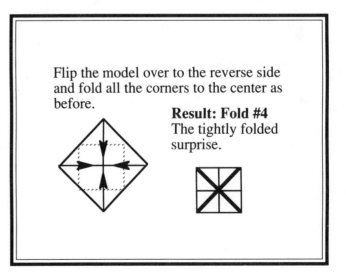

Flip the model over to the reverse side and fold all the corners to the center as before.

Result: Fold #4 The tightly folded surprise.

But look at this....*(Hold up fold #4)*. I don't think my mother will understand that this little square is actually a personalized Mother's Day gift...Hey! Wait a minute! She loves flowers. If I press my thumb in the middle like this *(demonstrate)* and peel up the points from underneath like this *(demonstrate)* then I can really surprise my mother. I've turned this plain square envelope into a beautiful lotus blossom that shows her exactly how special she really is!

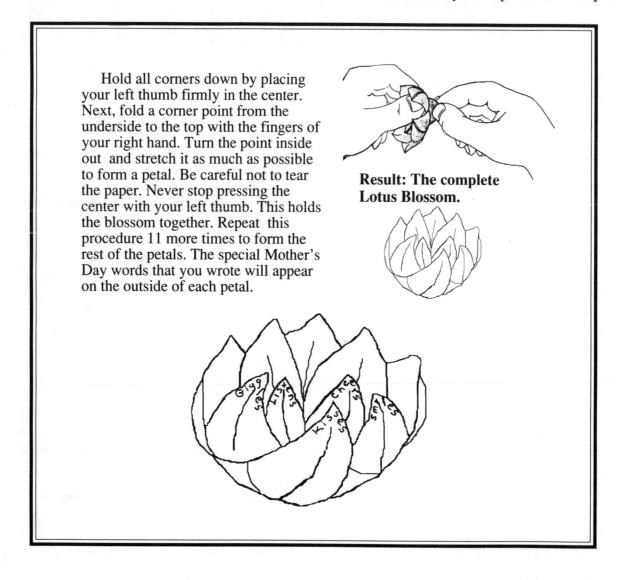

Hold all corners down by placing your left thumb firmly in the center. Next, fold a corner point from the underside to the top with the fingers of your right hand. Turn the point inside out and stretch it as much as possible to form a petal. Be careful not to tear the paper. Never stop pressing the center with your left thumb. This holds the blossom together. Repeat this procedure 11 more times to form the rest of the petals. The special Mother's Day words that you wrote will appear on the outside of each petal.

Result: The complete Lotus Blossom.

Summary of folding directions:

Preliminary folds: Fold a square in half along the vertical midline, then fold the resulting rectangle in half along the horizontal midline. Completely unfold for storytelling.

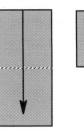

Write the words in the corners as shown, then fold all four corners to the center. Crease along the dotted lines.

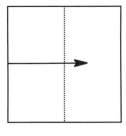

Result: Fold #1 The folded note about love for mother.

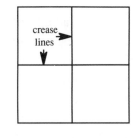

Write the words in the corners as before and fold the corners to the center.

Result: Fold #2 The second envelope.

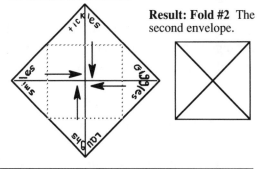

Write the words in the corners and fold them into the center as before. **Result: Fold #3** The third envelope.

Flip the model over to the reverse side and fold all the corners to the center as before.

Result: Fold #4 The tightly folded surprise.

Hold all corners down by placing your left thumb firmly in the center. Next, fold a corner point from the underside to the top with the fingers of your right hand. Turn the point inside out and stretch it as much as possible to form a petal. Be careful not to tear the paper. Never stop pressing the center with your left thumb. This holds the blossom together. Repeat this procedure 11 more times to form the rest of the petals. The special Mother's Day words that you wrote will appear on the outside of each petal.

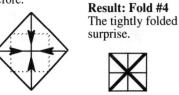

Result: The complete Lotus Blossom.

HOLIDAY HISTORY

How did Mother's Day traditions begin?

The earliest American attempts to establish a day set aside to honor mothers were made by Julia Ward Howe, the author of "The Battle Hymn of the Republic," and later, by Mary Towles Sasseen, a Kentucky teacher who sponsored annual music programs for mothers. Although these efforts resulted in scattered local support, the first nationally recognized Mother's Day was not observed until May 1907.

A school teacher named Anna M. Jarvis arranged a special mother's service in her church in Philadelphia to pay tribute to her deceased mother. Because her mother had been an avid gardener and loved sharing her flowers with others, she asked that white carnations be worn by all those attending. The next year, more churches held special Mother's Day services on the second Sunday in May. By 1911, the observance had spread to every state, as well as to Canada, Mexico, Europe, South America, Africa, China, and Japan. Leaflets suggesting activities for the services were printed in ten languages and distributed throughout the world.

A Mother's Day International Association was incorporated in 1912 to encourage even greater observance of the day. In May of 1913, the United States House of Representatives adopted a resolution calling upon the President, his Cabinet, the Senators and Representatives and all Federal officials to wear a white carnation on the second Sunday in May. On May 9, 1914, President Wilson issued the first Mother's Day Proclamation and designated the second Sunday in May as a day set aside to express "our love and reverence for the mothers of our country."

The custom of wearing white carnations was reserved for those whose mothers were dead. Those with living mothers wore red carnations. Soon the tradition of gift-giving emerged, and has grown more popular every year. The increasing commercialism and the addition of non-church related Mother's Day activities alarmed and dismayed Anne Jarvis, the woman responsible for promoting the holiday in America. She struggled to keep Mother's Day free from commercialism, but was increasingly unsuccessful. She became a bitter recluse and died at the age of 84, in a quiet sanitarium in West Chester, Pennsylvania. It is probable that Anne Jarvis would have approved of the simple, handmade, personalized origami lotus flower featured in "Mother's Day Surprise." It was store-bought cards and gifts that she disdained.

Although not connected to this holiday, the custom of honoring motherhood has existed since ancient times. Ancient Greeks worshipped Cybele, the mother of the gods, and ancient Romans sponsored the festival of Hilaria on the Ides of March. Early Christians celebrated Mothering Sunday on the fourth Sunday of Lent. The Church emphasized the concept of the Mother Church and encouraged worshippers to return to the church where they were baptized. The British version of Mother's Day is held on Mothering Sunday. Historically it was a day when servants and apprentices were allowed to "go a-mothering," to visit their homes and mothers.

Optional applications for "Mother's Day Surprise"

1. After telling the story, review the simple sequence for folding the lotus blossom *(auditory memory)*. Refold the flower for the group, using a fresh, unfolded square of paper *(visual memory)*. With such a thick and bulky model, it is important to emphasize the importance of firm and accurate creasing through all layers. Ask the group to demonstrate that they know the folding sequence by telling you exactly what to do, step-by-step. Discuss other words that individuals may want to substitute for the ones suggested in the story. Allow them to personalize their flowers, or simply use the words suggested. Some group members may want to draw instead of write, or connect the words into a short message or phrase. Ask the group to make three different lists containing four items that they want to include on their flowers. When the lists are complete, distribute squares of paper for individual folding *(kinesthetic memory)*.

Note: beginners often need practice in learning to reverse the petals. It is a common mistake to apply too much pressure and tear the paper. With an inexperienced group, it is advisable to make a practice blossom first, using a second or third attempt as an actual Mother's Day gift.

2. Research the importance of the lotus blossom in Eastern cultures. What other art forms use this symbol? What does it represent *(analysis)*?

3. Combine the group's individual models to make a single lotus blossom tree, mobile, sculpture, or string. Emphasize unity, friendship, and a sense of belonging within the group. Say, "We *all* made this together..." *(synthesis)*.

4. Use this activity with other themes, such as the meaning of patriotism, friendship, springtime, or religious holidays. Make lotus blossoms as farewell, birthday, or get-well gifts. Use personalized adjectives that describe the honorary person or event *(application)*.

5. Make a giant lotus blossom from 36" squares of wrapping paper or art paper. Present the story as a Mother's Day play, with several people assisting with the folds and lettering. Substitute "We" and "Our" for "I" and "My". Alternate narrators, or simply use one. As always, prefold the giant model up to fold #4. Do not peel back the petals ahead of time. With such a large piece of paper, it is possible to create more

layers, depending on the paper's bulkiness and the physical strength of the paperfolders *(synthesis)*.

6. Attach the blossom to round green paper symbolizing a lily pad. Spray with water-proofing material or laminate the leaf. Float in a clear container, or use as nametags, center pieces, as part of a Mother's Day display, or as place cards *(application)*.

7. Make different sizes to decorate cards or gifts. Create tiny lotus blossom earrings. String several tiny lotus blossoms together as a necklace. Use various colors. Experiment with a variety of paper weights and textures. Try folding one from fabric *(synthesis)*.

8. Establish a lotus blossom equation: if a 8.5" sq. makes a 3.5" flower, what size flower will a 10" sq. yield *(analysis)*?

Date	Group	Notes

For more information....

National Organizations

The following groups provide members with informative newsletters, sponsor annual conventions, special events and festivals, and compile complete lists of regional groups, materials, and resources. Membership is inexpensive and easily obtained by inquiring at the addresses listed below.

National Association for the Preservation and Perpetuation of Storytelling (NAPPS), P. O. Box 309, Jonesborough, TN 37659. Phone 615-753-2171.

The Friends of The Origami Center of America, 15 West 77 St., New York, NY 10024-5192. Phone 212-769-5635.

Other sources for material containing both paper folding and text:

Gross, Gay Merrill, 1991, *World of Crafts: Folding Napkins*, p. 117, New York, NY: Mallard Press.

Kallevig, Christine Petrell, 1991, *Folding Stories: Storytelling and Origami Together As One*, Newburgh, IN: Storytime Ink Intl.

Murry and Rigney, 1928, *Paper Folding For Beginners*, Dover.

Pellowski, Anne, 1987, *Family Storytelling Handbook*, p. 74-84 (two stories written by Gay Merrill Gross), New York, NY: Macmillan Publishing Co.

Rey, H. A., 1952, *Curious George Rides A Bike*, New York, NY: Houghton.

Schimmel, Nancy, 1982, *Just Enough To Make A Story: A Sourcebook For Storytellers*, p. 20-32, Berkeley, CA: Sisters' Choice Press.

Books for beginning paper folders:

Adair, Ian, 1975, *Papercrafts: Step by Step Series*, London: David & Charles Publishers.

Ayture-Scheele, Zulal, 1987, *The Great Origami Book,* New York, NY: Sterling Publishing Co.

Ayture-Scheele, Zulal, 1986, *Origami In Color: paperfolding fun,* New York, NY: Gallery Books.

Jackson, Paul, 1989, *The Complete Origami Course,* New York, NY: Gallery Books.

Kasahara, Kunihiko, 1973, *Origami Made Easy,* Tokyo, Japan: Japan Publication.

Kobayashi, Kazuo and Yamaguchi, Makoto, 1987, *Origami for Parties*, New York: Kodansha International.

Lewis, Shari and Oppenheimer, Lillian, 1962, *Folding Paper Puppets,* New York, NY: Stein and Day Publishers.

Lewis, Shari and Oppenheimer, Lillian, 1965, *Folding Paper Masks,* New York, NY: Dutton.

Randlett, Samuel, 1961, *The Best of Origami,* New York: E. P. Dutton & Co., Inc.

Sakata, Hideaki, *Origami*, New York: Kodansha International.

Sarasas, Claude, 1964, *The ABC's Of Origami,* Rutland, VT: Charles E. Tuttle, Inc.

Takahama, Toshie, 1985, *The Joy of Origami,* Tokyo, Japan: Shufunotomo/Japan Publications. (also by the same author: *Origami Toys, Origami for Fun, Quick and Easy Origami).*

Weiss, Stephen, 1984, *Wings & Things: origami that flies*, New York, NY: St. Martin's Press.

Books with historic information about origami:

Honda, Isao, 1965, *The World of Origami,* Rutland, VT: Japan Publications Trading Co.

Lang, Robert J., 1988, *The Complete Book of Origami*, New York, NY: Dover Publications, Inc.

Randlett, Samuel, 1961, *The Art of Origami,* New York, NY: E. P. Dutton & Co., Inc.

Books relating to storytelling techniques:

Greene, Ellin, *Storytelling: Art and Technique,* New York, NY: R. R. Bowker Co.

Herman, Gail, *Storytelling: A Triad in the Arts,* Mansfield Center, CT: Creative Learning Press.

Livo, Norma, *Storytelling: Process and Practice,* Englewood, CO: Libraries Unlimited.

Pellowski, Anne, 1987, *Family Storytelling Handbook,* New York, NY: Macmillan Publishing Co.

Schimmel, Nancy, 1982, *Just Enough To Make a Story: A Sourcebook For Storytelling*, Berkeley, CA: Sisters' Choice.

Christine Petrell Kallevig is available as a keynote speaker or to present Storigami demonstrations at conventions, workshops, assemblies, or festivals. Contact the publisher, Storytime Ink International, P. O. Box 470505, Broadview Heights, Ohio 44147, for details.

Holiday references

Appelbaum, Diana Karter, *Thanksgiving: an American Holiday, An American History*, 1984, Facts on File Publications, New York, NY.

Agel, Jerome and Shulman, Jason, *The Thanksgiving Book,* Dell Publishing Co., Inc., New York, NY.

Cardozo, Arlene Rossen, *Jewish Family Celebrations,* 1982, St. Martin's Press, New York, NY.

Cashman, Greer Fay and Frinkel, Alona, *Jewish Days and Holidays*, 1986, Adams Books, New York, NY.

Charing, Douglas, *The Jewish World,* 1983, Silver Burdett Company, Morristown, NJ.

Douglas, George William, *The American Book of Days,* 1937, The H. W. Wilson Company, New York, NY.

Cordello, Becky Stevens, *Celebrations,* 1977, Butterick Publishing, New York, NY.

Cuyler, Margery, *Jewish Holidays*, 1978, Holt, Rinehart & Winston, New York, NY.

D'Aulaire, Ingri and Edgar Parin, *Columbus*, 1955, Doubleday & Co., Inc., New York, NY.

Domnitz, Myer, *Judaism*, 1986, The Bookwright Press, New York, NY.

Dunkling, Leslie, *A Dictionary of Days: The Curious Stories Behind More Than 850 Named Days Celebrated in Literature and Real Life,* Facts on File Publications, New York, NY.

Foley, Dan, *Toys Through The Ages,* 1962, Chilton Books, Philadelphia, PA.

Gaer, Joseph, *Holidays Around The World,* 1953, Little, Brown and Company, Boston, MA.

Gibbons, Gail, *Things To Make And Do For Columbus Day,* 1977, Franklin Watts, New York, NY.

Gleiter, Jan and Thompson, Kathleen, *Christopher Columbus,* 1987, Raintree Children's Books, Milwaukee, WI.

Greene, Carol, *Christopher Columbus*, 1989, Children's Press, Chicago, IL.

Hannum, Dotti, *Thanksgiving Handbook,* 1985, The Child's World, Inc.

Herda, D. J.,*Halloween,* Franklin Watts, New York, NY.

Hierstein-Morris, Jill, *Halloween: Facts and Fun*, 1988, Creatively Yours Publications, Ankeny, IA.

Hildebrandt, Greg, *Treasures of Chanukah,* 1987, The Unicorn Publishing House, Morris Plains, NJ.

Hoff, Carol, *Holidays and History,* 1967, Steck-Vaughn Company, Austin, TX.

Hole, Christina, *Easter and Its Customs,* 1961, M. Barrows and Company, New York, NY.

Ickis, Marguerite, *The Book of Festival Holidays,* 1964, Dodd, Mead & Co., New York, NY.

Krythe, Maymie R., *All About American Holidays,* 1962, Harper & Brothers, Publishers, New York, NY.

Matthews, Rupert, *The Voyage of Columbus*, 1989, The Bookwright Press, New York, NY.

McSpadden, J. Walker, *The Book of Holidays*, 1958, Thomas Y. Crowell Co., New York, NY.

Metcalfe, Edna, *The Trees of Christmas,* 1969, Abingdon Press, Nashville, TN.

Morison, Samuel Eliot, *Admiral of the Ocean Sea, a life of Christopher Columbus, Vol. 1 & 2,* 1942, Boston, Little, Brown and Company.

Morison, Samuel Eliot, *The European Discovery of America, The Southern Voyages,* 1974, Oxford University Press, New York, NY.

Nickerson, Betty, *Celebrate the Sun*, 1969, J. B. Lippincott Company, Philadelphia, PA.

Perry, Margaret, *Holiday Magic,* 1978, Doubleday & Co., Garden City, NY.

Purdy, Susan Gold, *Jewish Holidays: Facts, Activities and Crafts*, 1969, J. B. Lippincott Company, Philadelphia, PA.

Rockland, Mae Shafter, *The Hanukkah Book,* 1975, Schocken Books, Inc., New York, NY.

Rockland, Mae Shafter, *The Jewish Party Book,* 1978, Schocken Books, Inc., New York, NY.

Sale, Kirkpatrick, *The Conquest of Paradise,* 1990, Alfred A. Knopf, New York, NY.

Sandak, Cass R., *Columbus Day,* 1990, Crestwood House, Macmillan Publishing Co., New York, NY.

Secrist, Elizabeth Hough, *Red Letter Days,* 1965, MaCrae Smith Company, Philadelphia, PA.

Shenkman, Richard, *Legends, Lies & Cherished Myths of American History,* 1988, William Morrow and Company, New York, NY.

Soule, Gardner, *Christopher Columbus: On the Green Sea of Darkness*, 1988, Franklin Watts, New York, NY.

Tuleja, Tad, *Curious Customs: The Stories Behind 296 Popular American Rituals,* 1987, Crown Publishers, Inc. New York, NY.

Walker, Mark, *The Great Halloween Book,* 1983, Liberty Publishing Company, Cockeysville, Md.

Glossary

Activity Therapy: A general category that usually encompasses music therapy, art therapy, dance therapy, recreational therapy, and occupational therapy. These therapies are generally found in psychiatric, rehabilitation, nursing, or educational centers.

Analysis: A thinking skill related to the ability to reason, decipher consequences, or determine procedural steps or components.

Auditory memory: Thoughts, information, or experiences derived through hearing or listening.

Application: A thinking skill related to the ability to use knowledge, information, or techniques in a practical manner.

Bloom's Taxonomy: A system developed by Benjamin S. Bloom *(Taxonomy of Educational Objectives, Handbook I: Cognitive Domain, New York: David McKay Co., Inc., 1956)* that organizes educational objectives into two basic realms, cognitive and affective. The cognitive hierarchy starts with knowledge and then progresses to comprehension, application, analysis, synthesis and evaluation. The higher order thought processes (analysis, synthesis, and evaluation) are of major concern when promoting children's abilities to function as independent, effective thinkers.

Evaluation: A thinking skill related to the ability to make judgements, make decisions, or set criteria based on a combination of observed data and probable consequences.

Fine motor coordination: The ability to integrate information derived from the senses (sight, sound, tactile) with small motions of the fingers and hands. Folding origami is an example.

Folklore: Traditions, beliefs, stories, and art forms preserved by a culture's common people, often using oral teaching techniques within the family social structure. Origami and storytelling are both examples.

Gami *(kami):* A Japanese word meaning paper.

Irony: A literary technique where the outcome is different or opposite from what may be expected.

Kinesthetic memory: Thoughts, information, or experiences derived through actions or tactile sensations.

Left brain: Refers to the left lobe of the cerebral cortex, generally considered to be the site of analysis, word processing, and linear and sequential thought processes. Understanding a sequence of story events is an example.

Mountain folding: A basic origami folding technique which results in a tent-like or mountain shaped fold, as in fold #1 on page 35.

Multi-sensory: Receiving input or information from several senses at the same time.

Ori: A Japanese word meaning folded.

Origami: Paper folding techniques preserved and developed through Japanese folklore, generally involving the folding of paper into two or three dimensional figures without cutting and gluing. It has now spread throughout the world and includes thousands of creative and traditional models. *Origami* also refers to the folded figure itself, i.e., the folded rabbit is an origami.

Right brain: Refers to the right lobe of the cerebral cortex, generally considered to be the site of emotions, artistic talent, intuition, and abstract, holistic thought processes. Imagining the shape of the final origami figure is an example.

Spatial relations: Refers to how a particular object is aligned in space in reference to a fixed point, such as one's body.

Storigami: A term coined by Christine Petrell Kallevig (*Folding Stories: Storytelling and Origami Together As One, Storytime Ink Intl., Newburgh, IN, 1991*) to describe the concept of combining storytelling and origami by illustrating stories with progressive origami folds.

Synthesis: A thinking skill related to creating, designing, or composing new thoughts or objects.

Valley folding: A basic origami technique resulting in a valley shaped fold, as in fold #1 on page 21.

Visual memory: Thoughts, information, or experiences derived through seeing or watching.

Visualization: The ability to imagine so clearly that one can "see" something in one's mind.

Whole brain: Refers to learning techniques which utilize both the right and left hemispheres of the cerebral cortex, resulting in greater memory retention and more rapid learning.

Index

Other items available from: STORYTIME INK International

Folding Stories: Storytelling and Origami Together As One by Christine Petrell Kallevig: Nine original short stories illustrated by nine easy origami models for ages preschool through adult. Includes extensive ideas for optional activities, complete illustrations and directions, photographs, glossary, and index. Recommended for storytellers, teachers, paperfolders, activity therapists or directors, and recreation leaders.
ISBN 0-9628769-0-9

Sunday Folding Stories: Storytelling and Origami Together For Sunday School Fun by Christine Petrell Kallevig: Original Sunday school stories illustrated by easy origami models, for ages preschool through adult. The stories are based on religious holidays and problem solving techniques using moral values. Includes dozens of suggestions for optional activities, complete illustrations and directions, photographs, and index.
ISBN 0-9628769-4-1

Pre-folded origami models, complete with instructions and Japanese origami paper: The origami models featured in **Folding Stories**, **Holiday Folding Stories**, and **Sunday Folding Stories** are pre-folded in richly colored origami paper. Package includes an instruction booklet and 36 sheets of origami paper in assorted colors and sizes.

Use this coupon to order additional copies of *Holiday Folding Stories: Storytelling and Origami Together For Holiday Fun*, or any of the other popular items *(library patrons - please photocopy)*.

Name_____

Address_____

City/State_____

Zip_____

item	Qty.	Price	Total
Folding Stories: Storytelling & Origami Together As One		$11.50	
Folding Stories pre-folded model kit		$9.50	
Holiday Folding Stories: Storytelling & Origami Together For Holiday Fun		$11.50	
Holiday Stories pre-folded model kit		$9.50	
Sunday Folding Stories: Storytelling & Origami Together For Sunday School Fun		$11.50	
Sunday Stories pre-folded model kit		$9.50	
		SUBTOTAL	
OH residents add 7% sales tax			
Postage & handling: Add $2 (1st item), $1 @ additional item			
US dollars only TOTAL ENCLOSED			

Mail to:
Storytime Ink International
P. O. Box 470505
Broadview Heights, OH 44147-0505

Allow 4 - 6 weeks for delivery